EDDY BRIMSON

Cover Design: Douglas Cheape.

Cover Photograph: Trudy Stade.

Created with Vellum

This novella is dedicated to all those that have supported me throughout my career. I have been incredibly lucky to have you there. Thank you one and all.

Especially mum.

ACKNOWLEDGMENTS

I would like to add a special note of gratitude to my brother Bob Brimson, and my great friend Douglas Cheape for all their help, advice, and encouragement in the making of *NAUGHTY BOY*, the one man play. I cannot overstate their importance to the play's ultimate success. I am profoundly grateful.

I must also add my thanks to Mark Rivlin, my sub editor. I also relinquish him of any blame for the strange grammar I insist stayed in.

And finally, to Lou, for the final push, and the ever-supportive Caimh and Elaine for their help.

INTRODUCTION

A few years back I was asked to write a screenplay for Lionsgate Films based around football and football violence. And so, the long journey of *Naughty Boy* began.

Writing a screenplay was a new and exciting opportunity for me, however, I quickly made the decision not to tread the same path as previous films on the subject, but rather try and focus on something far more interesting. I wanted to explore what it is that draws men towards such acts of violence. The first draft I delivered was deemed to be a bit to "arthouse" for their liking, and so I tucked it away and cracked on. However, once 'Kaz from marketing' suggested I introduce a love interest to the third draft, I knew my days were numbered ... I am not a fan of people like Kaz.

A good few years later whilst clearing out some

files on the PC, the original draft of that script popped up on the monitor. I gave it a quick read and felt that within the dialogue there may well be a decent book hiding, one that was not purely about football, but much more. I wanted to explore mental health, loyalty, love, violence, and loss. As well as looking into the way society appears to mould and shape us. And of course, the darker side I believe we all have hidden deep within. And so once again I set to work. Now, for those of you interested in writing I offer this advice; Do not do things arse about face. Going from screenplay to novel is hard work. Really hard work. In fact, you might as well just tuck it away and start afresh. And so, I did. Well, for the most part.

Alongside the book, I also found myself having to write a new comedy show for the Edinburgh Festival, when it struck me that within the books text there could well be a half decent play, and so once again I started another rewrite.

Now, as a comedian I am pretty much scripted. However, at the Festival I do like to step out of my comfort zone and do a bit of the weird stuff, as you are given more time to play in a show than you are in a normal club setting. For example, the grand finale to one year's offering saw me ending the show dressed in a white paper suit and wearing a gas mask. I then climbed out of the three-story window, whilst telling the crowd I was ending my career; 'As they were the best audience I'd ever had, and it could never get better than this.' I then closed the curtains and waited, perched on the window ledge until they had all left - As I said, the weird stuff. However, one night a woman was so convinced I was going to jump, that she tried to pull me back in. The pull and tug battle that ensured very nearly made her fear a reality, as I was left clinging to the curtain whilst those in the Grassmarket below applauded, thinking I was some kind of circus act. Still, at least I'd have made the papers. And believe me, at the Festival that is worth its weight in gold, even if it is an obituary.

The reason I relay that story is that for me the Festival is a place for experimenting and stepping out of the comfort zone, and writing a play offered me that opportunity. At first I thought of using four other comedians to play the characters, however that idea soon hit the rails due to comedians being notoriously hard to nail down - And what I mean by that is, lazy and unreliable. My next move was to make it a double header, sourcing proper actors to play all the parts, but once again I quickly found out that most actors are, for the most part, flaky and unreliable. And so, if it were to happen there was only one option left open to me. In truth it should have been the first. One of the reasons I got into stand-up is that it is totally down to you as an individual. If you fail, there is no one else to blame. No one can pull the rug from under you or take credit for your part in a body of work. As a comedian you swim alone, you sink alone. And so once again it was sink or swim time.

The play had its first airing in the basement of a pub in Glasgow. I was meant to be previewing the comedy show I was writing, along with one other comedian, JoJo Sutherland. However, with just four punters and one other comic, the lovely Viv Gee in the crowd, I felt the big showstopper I had planned in stripping down to just a crash helmet, pants and bra would make all present feel more than a little awkward. And so rather than pull the gig I asked if they would mind me trying out the play. It was their choice. I was either going to get my tits out or the words. Thankfully, they chose the words.

At this point you need to know that I had never attempted anything like that before. I would never have called myself an actor, though performing comedy is clearly an act. In fact, comedy is the purest artform of them all, despite the arts council refusal to both properly fund, or acknowledge it. Performing *Naughty Boy* certainly provided the challenge I was looking for. However, from day one my main focus has been the writing rather than the performance. It was a nerve-wracking experience, but incredibly rewarding. One of the great things about comedy is that it is immediate. You find out very quickly if a joke or routine works. The golden rule with comedy is, that if after three outings a joke still does not hit, then you bin it, and you write something new. Fine with a thirty second joke, or three-minute routine, but a fifty-minute play? This was new territory. I had no idea if the writing was any good but having already committed a few grand to putting it on at the Festival there was no turning back. Thankfully both JoJo and Viv told me that I was onto something.

The second time I performed the play was at 3:15pm on the opening afternoon of the 2019 Edinburgh Festival. There were three people in the audience. However, unlike stand-up it did not matter. This was something new. I was telling a story, not chasing laughs. And those three people, they stayed afterwards, and they told me they loved it. Word soon spread, and then the reviews started to appear, all rewarding the piece with either five or four stars. There was praise for the performance, but what pleased me most were the comments given to the words. Audiences got up to forty, half decent for Edinburgh, and the punters they continued to stay, and they wanted to talk. Many with questions they wanted answering. Each taking something different from the piece. *Naughty Boy*, the play, had far exceeded my expectations. And so, once the Festival was over, I revisited the book.

The style of the play changed the way I read it. I wanted it to be much closer to the live version, and so I started to cut it back. One of the most important books I have ever read is *Why I Write,* by *George Orwell.* Within it, he explains that every single word must count. That is the most important lesson I have ever learned regards writing. It guides my comedy, and so it should my fiction.

The original book version was padded out. I did not want that. Orwell's instruction is so important, and so the piece quickly reduced from sixty-five thousand words to what it has become, a novella of just under twenty-five thousand. That is some stripping back. But it shows just who much padding there was. For reference, the play at Edinburgh was limited to a fifty-minute slot and therefore came in at just under ten thousand words.

Naughty Boy, both the play and this novella, have proved to be a real lesson in life. There is a perception, particularly in TV land, that once you pass the age of forty you are done. This is of course bullshit. Creativity does not end.

I love being a comedian, it is not a job, it is a lifestyle. One in which you can tell a punter to f-off if they are being a pain in the arse. It is a path that has taken me around the world more than once. And I have met some of the most amazingly brilliant, stupid, and inspiring people you could ever hope to meet. But *Naughty Boy* taught me something else: Trust yourself to push yourself. It is never too late to try something new.

I am immensely proud of both this novella and the play. I honestly think it is the best thing I have ever created. It is the start of the next chapter.

I hope you enjoy it.

Eddy

DISCLAIMER

Please keep in mind that this is a work of fiction.

Some of the character names within the story do relate to personal friends, though once again the scenarios in which they appear are fictional and purely coincidental ... Well, I say that ...

Eddy

If you would like some music to get you in the mood, then I recommend: *Newtown Aces.*

1

Welcome to my world, the ward. This, my friend, is where the heads rock and the marbles roll. This is where the ravers hang out. Only there is no amount of Paracetamol or Red Bull that will clear any of these heads, because these are the raving mad, the Freaks, the Schizos and the Mongs. And this, this place, this is where they hide them away.

Take him, there at the window, ducking and diving with each passing bird. He's a former Catholic priest. Poor fella lost his mum in the London terror attacks – sent him doolally. He's now so convinced they're out to get him as well that he's even tried to disguise himself as one of them. I mean, that is some beard on the fella, eh!

'Are you alright there Father?'

'They'll have us all sucking on dogs' cocks if we don't convert, Joe!'

'Well it'd make a change from sucking off choir-boys, eh! Now, do you want the soup or the fish?'

'What kind of fish is it?'

'I don't know! Fish fish!'

What kind of fish is it for fuck's sake! I give him the fish. And I move on.

'Prick. Wanker. Knob jockey.'

That'll be Ron, shouting at the telly, just as he always does. It'll be the news. It's always the news for some reason. Fuck knows why! Probably some scumbag politician expertly answering none of the questions he – or she for that matter – is being asked. Still you know what they say, 'You get what you vote for'. And when I say *You,* I do mean *You*. I don't vote for those cunts!

'Arsehole, wanky, fuck nose.'

'Go on Ron, you tell 'em, mate.'

'Joe stop it. Don't encourage him.'

'Sorry nurse, but he's funny ain't he? I said Ron, he's funny?'

'I said don't encourage him. And Ron, be quiet. What's wrong with you?'

'What's wrong with him?' ... Now there's a daft question if ever there was. Because there's clearly plenty wrong with young Ronnie there, eh! I mean, look at the bloody state of him!

That said, we've all got a bit of wrong in us, ain't we? You. Me. That fella you pass on the way to work every day. Because it's a fine line we tread. Each and every one of us. A very, fine, line.

I mean, don't tell me you've never wanted to shout in the face of someone, some *prick* you know is constantly turning you over. Or that while out driving your car, you've never had that sudden urge to just veer off the road into a bus stop packed with mums, kids, and old dears, and just wipe the fuckers out. Each and every one of them, just like that, while all along knowing you could be happily on your way. Or that while in a restaurant, sat opposite the one you love. Where the food is perfect. And the wine is like nectar. That you've never once looked up into those eyes opposite, those eyes that melted your heart, and from somewhere suddenly thought to yourself: - *'I could stab you right in the fucking neck with this fork.'* - I mean, we've all had those thoughts, right? That's just, normal!

So let's not go getting too judgy with this lot in here. Because they're not wrong 'uns as such, eh. Not proper wrong 'uns. I mean, they're not nonces, or murderers, or some scumbag politician out for him or herself. This lot in here, well they're just not well, that's all. Their wiring's a bit fucked up. Some of this lot don't know the fish from the soup, should they have enough about them to even make that choice! And do you know what, there but for the grace of

God, and all that. If of course you believe in God? Or any of the other imaginary friends so many hide behind as an excuse to mask the true madness of this world.

I push on past the ward sister's office. The door is open, as it is most of the time, and I see her there, head buried in her work:

'Afternoon sister.'

She looks up, but not back, and checks the clock above her head:

'So it is! Afternoon Joe.'

She's sexy, the ward sister. She has to be fifty if she's a day, but she's a very good-looking woman. And she wears her uniform tight to show off her curves. Not that I've noticed, of course. And she's dyed her hair darker. It suits her.

I move on. And I go about my business. Uni, a small Japanese woman - I think - is up and buzzing about. She's always on the move is Uni, the meds don't seem to slow her down. Though I guess the docs would give her something if they thought she was a threat. To herself that is. Or anyone else for that matter. I watch as she hands out invisible presents to those sitting stupefied, or just still, before the wall-mounted television. Most are oblivious, though some receive their gifts with puzzled grace. Others are less impressed:

'Happy birthday Nigel.'

He snatches the imaginary offering and throws it to the floor:

'It's not my birthday!'

He then kicks out at her shins but misses. Another guest, as they like to call them these days, laughs. Nigel grabs whatever it was, or wasn't, from the floor and throws it at him forcing the man to wince. Unlike Uni, Nigel could probably do with a bit more calming. That said I like Nigel. He's a fucking loon, but he's got some fight in him. I admire that, a bit of fight. Nigel may be bonkers, but he won't just sit there and take it.

It was on my tenth birthday that dad first took me, some kind of present I suppose. Or maybe he saw it as a day of reckoning. Who knows? Strange that it was my old man rather than any of the others that took me. Well, took us really, what with him being such a quiet, gentle fella. Maybe he was different when he was younger, though I can't see it.

They wouldn't let any of us in the ring until we'd been going a year. A stupid rule, I thought, a whole year! I mean you've either got it in you, or you haven't, eh? Might as well just get on with it I say.

And then the night finally came, four days after my eleventh birthday. And they chucked me in, though I was more than happy in going. The other lad was older and bigger. And his fists, they were faster. It was cruel really, I mean he must have been thirteen, the other lad. He was built like that anyway. Well that's how it seemed to me, at the time. And as I say, there was me, eleven years and four days. And that's a big gap at that age, those two years. A big gap. If indeed he was thirteen! And I was taking a proper beating, I was. My head being knocked all over the shop. From here to there, from right, from left, clump, clump, clump. Until eventually I was knocked to my arse. And so the trainer, the one that chucked me in with the older lad to start with, also chucked in the towel:

'That'll learn ya son. You gotta keep them hands up, or else you'll always end up down 'ere, you hear?'

I remember the wry smile on his lips. That smile, forever imprinted upon me. Happy with the lesson he'd dealt out:

'Now let's get those gloves off.'

Laughter spun around my head as those lining the ring praised the older lad. I pulled myself back to my feet. And as the trainer went for the laces, something from somewhere deep inside, told me I wasn't quite done:

'Let me have another go. Go on, just one more minute?'

My words took the trainer by surprise. And they forced the smile on that face of his wider still. Nasty bastard that he was:

'Okay then, on you go. But remember, keep those hands up.'

In a show of bravado, I slapped my gloves together,

as I'd seen boxers do. Proper boxers. *Real* boxers. I bounced on my toes, full of myself I was - eleven years and four days. The older lad, eager for more, drew close. We touched gloves, as boxers do. And as those that had laughed looked on, I then launched a boot straight into his bollocks, bollocks that had probably not long dropped. If indeed they had at all, for he was only thirteen - I think? He fell to the floor doubled in pain, his screams echoing around the hall. And as he writhed there at my feet:

'Fucking clump me like that you fucking cunt.'

Huh, *'Cunt!'* And there was me, eleven years and four days! The trainer shoved me back against the ropes, but the tongue-lashing he spat my way fell on deaf ears, my eyes firmly fixed on that lad, that older lad:

'Think you're 'ard do ya. Fucking prick.'

Moments later I burst through the doors of that boxing club and out into a side alley, the angry trainer giving chase, until eventually he pulled up, hands on knees, gasping for air. And with the chase over, I turned, I spread my arms out wide and yelled at the top of my voice: 'WANKERRRRRR.'

Now there's a pose I've come to both know and love. But come on! I mean, the nerve of that lad, just clump, clump, clumping away at me like that! But from that moment on: *'He's a wrong 'un that Joe, a proper wrong 'un I tell ya!'* And, you know what they say, if you fling enough shit, well, eventually some might just stick eh! Me, a wrong 'un! Funny that, when you think about it. Especially in a place such as this!

I deliver fish here and soup there. Unlike the priest most don't even ask, they just accept what is dished out to them. Though I still offer them the choice. Well, it would be rude not to. But most have other things on their mind.

Take that girl there, the one with the blond hair doing the jigsaw, Karen, Karen's her name. To look at, she appears as normal as you or I. But if you stand and watch long enough, they'll come a moment when she thinks no-one is looking. She'll not turn to check mind, but when she *thinks* no-one is looking. And she'll take a piece of that jigsaw, pop it down the front of her knickers, and push it up her fanny. Weird, eh! That said, there'll be plenty outside of these pale blue walls. People in both high and low places with far stranger quirks and perversions than young Karen's. Only, they know to keep it hidden! Well most do! And fuck it, it's her fanny, she can do what she likes with it! That said it's not her jigsaw, so swings and roundabouts.

And then of course there are the ones you can spot a mile off, like young Suzie there, her hair matted to her head. It's the meds that does it. They make them sweaty. As ever Susie sits there trapped, staring straight ahead. At what, only she knows. For some reason I'm one of the few that can get through to her. I'll show you:

'You alright there Suzie?'

She turns and smiles me her smile. Spit strings her lips, and then she offers up her arms.

'You want a cuddle? 'Ere, come here, I'll give you a cuddle, sweetheart.'

It's not too much to ask is it, a cuddle, a little bit of love? I had a lot of love growing up. A lot of love. Worth remembering that, the love you had as a kid, if indeed you were lucky enough to have any that is. I was lucky, I had a lot of love. Maybe mum or dad should have slapped me about a bit. Maybe that would have sorted me out. Although I doubt it, because you see the thing is, I don't mind getting the odd slap, never have done. It makes me feel – *alive!* The old man has never laid a finger on me, bless him. What with him being the way he is, a gentle fella I mean. Mum did, mind! Oh yeah, she hit me. Just the once. But she did. Sixteen I was. Huh! It took me that long to break her!

Now obviously being sixteen, I was the most important person on the planet. I knew everything about everything. And as long as I had enough socks to knock one out into, everything was turning out just as I wanted. Socks and a clean shirt that is! I mean, a young lad's got to have a clean shirt, eh! If he's going out I mean! A clean shirt? Well you'd think so wouldn't ya!

I remember it clear as day. I'd come home from

work, my first job, picking weeds out of the bunkers at the local golf course. One less for the dole queue. And there she was as I walked up the hallway, her back to me, standing at the sink. Mum. Dear old mum:

'Alright mum? I'm going out tonight, iron me a shirt will ya? And make sure it's a clean one. Because you never know, I might get lucky, eh!'

'Hello love. I'll iron you one, but I'm not sure you've got any clean, I've not done a wash today.'

'What do ya mean you've not done a wash?'

'I've not done a wash love, I've not had time.'

'You've not had time! What do you mean, you've not had time? What the fuck do you do all day?'

Now with hindsight, I realise that was a bad choice of words. Because as it turned out my mum clearly spent a good part of her day practising her right hook. Bloody good 'un an' all, it was. No wonder the old man never answered her back, he must have been scared shitless. poor bastard!

I left home that day.

Well I say that, I actually legged it across the road to my best mate Dave's house. And we laughed and we joked. And we listened to music, drank beer, and played darts. And I stayed. And I waited. I waited until the lights were out back home, and I'd seen she'd gone to bed. And then I snuck back in. Cruel really. Because I know she'd have been crying all night, *hitting her poor little soldier like that!* And of course once back, there on the bed was a freshly washed, beautifully pressed, nice clean shirt, right there waiting for me. Only it was too late by then, weren't it! Because I never did get to go out. And who knows what might have happened on that night? That night of all my nights on this earth. For that could have been it, my one and only chance. The night my eyes were destined to fall upon the one that would have brought me to my knees. The one that would have such a hold on me that I'd give my life for her. That night. That one night, of all my nights. The one I would love, cherish, and obey. The one whom I would nurse or be nursed by until our final breath. The one who grew into the woman that would have carried our children and made me the man I was meant to be, rather than the one I've become. That one night of all my nights, might have been my one and only chance.

But no, I never did get to go out. And all because mum didn't wash a shirt. Some cheap piece of cotton stitched together by the bleeding fingers of some poor bastard in China, or wherever the fuck it was made. Some poor cunt doing their best to make ends meet. Just to survive. Working every godforsaken hour just to put food on the table of those they themselves would die for. Someone who'd give his right bollock, or her right tit to be cracking jokes, listening to music, drinking beer and chucking arrows with their best mate, in a bedroom, in a land far, far away, without a care in the world. While all the time knowing, *knowing,* that a shout down the stairs to Dave's dear old mum would not only bring a smile, and a sandwich, but one more of those beautiful, golden, ice cold beers to wash it all down with. But no! I never did get to go out. And all because mum didn't put a wash on. Mums, eh! You've got to love your fucking mum.

'Shitty fuck arse face!

'Ha ... Go on Ron. You tell 'em.'

I had the odd whack at school of course, mainly from the headmaster. Fella called Sutton. Nasty, vicious cunt of a man. Local magistrate. God help ya if you ended up in his court. But that's about all I did take from that place, the odd whack. There wasn't much hope or ambition instilled in me, or any of the others with whom I shared *the best days of my life*. That said they were good days for the most part. They were, good days.

The sad reality is that they got most of us just as they wanted us. Designed for life. Fleshy ill-educated little cogs churned out to keep the wheels of the machine chug, chug, chugging along, just the way it's meant to. Because they need the likes of us, those that feed off us. They need the likes of you and me to do their dirty work. Without us they are fucked! And we'd do well to remember that. To understand our worth. To value ourselves more than they ever will, rather than just accepting our role, our *place*.

I don't blame the teachers, poor bastards. Well, not all of them anyway. Looking back on it their hands were tied as much as ours. Our heads just happened to pop out of the wrong hole, simple as that.

The only silver spoon we had came in white bags from the local supermarket or the corner shop. It sweetened our tea and rotted our teeth. There were some good teachers, of course. Decent people who gave their best, despite the shackles placed upon them: *'Prove them wrong'*, they'd say. *'Go forth and prove the bastards wrong. You're as good as any'*. Beautiful proud words offered up by good, honest people. Maybe that's why I am here on the ward, at the sharp end so to speak. Dishing out meals. Watching arses get wiped. And mopping up the sick of people who are just as likely to smash their heads through the windows as they are to ask for a bowl of soup, some love, or a jigsaw to push up inside themselves.

'Shitty stick. Tit fuck.'

On the television I notice footage from some refugee camp in fuck knows where. Children with lost, innocent looks on their faces. Men with guns, both the good and the bad, though which is which is open to interpretation. So much suffering and yet so much money to be made. War! What, or rather *who* is it good for? Certainly not the likes of you or me. Or any of those lost, innocent faces that had moments ago stared out, but are now gone. Brushed aside so that we can be told the weather: - *'I wonder if it'll be hot tomorrow?'* - Like it matters to any of those in here. Or any of those children. Some of whom by the time those images arrived, may well be gone forever.

'Fuuuucky prick ball sack.'

'Ron, calm down.'

The nurse doesn't even look his way, but others are starting to rock back and forth in their seats, laughing, egging Ron on:

'Knob sucker. Wanky tit fuck.'

'I said calm down!'

I'm one of Thatcher's children. Evil, war mongering whore of a woman. I'll piss on her grave before my days are done, I swear I will. I will find the hole that keeps her under and I will piss upon it. She, more than any other in my time, turned us in on each other. Greed is good, she told us. The me, me, me generation: *'You must have this. You must have that'*. 'But why?' *'Because she has it, he has it. Do not get left behind!'* But where has their greed got us, eh? Nowhere, that's where. Greed does nothing but destroy us, because ultimately, it's a tool to control and divide us. And like fools to this day we continue to buy into it. And they drip feed us shit we don't need, to replace the perfectly good stuff we already have. So, you end up spending money you can ill afford. And then you borrow to keep up. And then you borrow again to stop yourself from going under, and then, well then they've got you ain't they! They've got you. They're clever fuckers, I'll give 'em that, those so desperate to control us. They are, clever, fuckers!

'Cock prick fuck face, shitty shit stinkers.

'Go on Ronny boy.'

But make no mistake, they need us. Oh, do they need us! More than they would ever dare let us know. Take this place. This place stinks of piss. Piss and disinfectant, and it's hidden away. It's hidden because there's not many that want to see this. There's not many that want to face up to the reality of what's not quite right. But thank fuck there are some, that there are *some* who set their greed aside. And who love, who give, and who care. Because where would they be without them, eh? Where would they be without these white and blue-cottoned angels who walk silently across these floors in their soft-soled shoes? Lost, that's where. Up a shitty creek without a paddle to push the turds aside. Not that those turds ever come here of course.

'Greedy cock suck. Arse shit.'

'Go on Ronnie son.'

'Right that's enough!'

Oh, Oh! That's the ward sister. That'll be the end of that.

'But he's funny eh, sister?'

'And that goes for you too Joe. Stop encouraging him. Now, everyone just sit still, watch the television and be quiet. Or else it goes off and it's all back to your rooms.'

Fair enough, I suppose. She fixes the room with that stare of hers. A stare laced with kindness and compassion, and she stands there for a count of one ... two ... three ... four ... five ... And with that she turns to leave. But as she goes, Ron being Ron, well, he just can't help himself now can he:

'Mingey, tit face, titty, moooooo cow.

She stops, but she dare not turn. Though the jiggle in her shoulders clearly gives her laughter away:

'I said, that's enough!'

'But he is funny eh sister? You've got to admit, Ron, he's funny!'

And then another voice starts to fill my head.

'Nurrrr Nurrr. Nooo.'

Her muffled groans mix with the shrill cut of a chair leg as it scrapes the polished floor.

'Now sit still and take your medication.'

I stop and I watch as Jenny, a small skeleton of a woman, clamps her lips so tightly they begin to turn blue.

'Open your mouth and ...'

An arm flies up, catching the nurse full in the face. I watch as she staggers back, the metallic taste of blood on her tongue alarming her senses. Now free, Jenny pulls herself up. The nurse, fuelled by a mix of anger and pain grabs for her, desperate to force her back down. But with madness comes great strength - something you learn quickly in places like this. And I stand and I watch as the nurse calls for back-up:

'I need some help here.'

Her cry alerts the ward sister. A bell begins to ring and the rest of the *guests* instantly fall silent. Some turn away. Others stand. All, including Ron, now oblivious to the television.

'Quick, I need help here.'

And I watch as Jenny's arms swing this way and that. Suddenly the nurse buckles. The crack of her nose shooting a message to her brain, as well as mine. And I wince: – *'That's going to hurt, that.'* - I think. Well I know. I can tell, because of the blood now dripping over her lips, wetting her chin and down to the floor: – *'Going to take some cleaning, that.'* - Releasing her grip, the nurse stumbles backwards, offering Jenny the freedom she craves, but in pulling herself up once more, Jenny knocks her chair to the floor and the metal legs become entangled with her own. She trips, and then falls. Her head cracks the side of the table. The smack of the polished floor then brings a second shattering blow. And I stand and I watch, like the others, transfixed. A young doctor races into the room, followed by a porter. Blood pours from Jenny's head, the thick crimson staining the polished grey flooring: – *'Now that really is a mess.'* - I think to myself. A fit takes hold, as it often does in this place. Her spasms smear her blood, diluting its colour a beautiful shade of pink. And the doctor barks:

'FOR CHRIST'S SAKE GRAB HOLD OF HER.'

And I stand. And I watch. And then I can't help but wonder: - *'Is he shouting at me? Well he better fucking not be!'*

'DON'T JUST STAND THERE. HELP.'

A nurse pushes past, forcing me aside. They pin poor Jenny to the floor and force a needle deep inside her skin. And in my head I count - as you learn to do in places such as this for ... one ... two ... three ... four ... right up to ... fifteen or thereabouts. And then Jenny, poor, poor Jenny, stills her shaking body.

'Jesus Joe! What the hell were you doing just standing there? You could see she was having a fit.'

And I realise: – *'He was. He was shouting at me. Well fuck me, there's a turn-up!'* - Because the thing is, grabbing hold of people like that, like they do, well, that's not my job now is it! I mean: - *'I could get in trouble for that.'* – And suddenly I find my eyes fixed on his, on that doctor fella. And I could feel it rising from deep within:

'No, no mate. Don't you go shouting at me...'

I could feel the anger boiling up ...

'Don't you EVER shout at me, you hear? You shout at me an' I'll FUCKING ...'

The porter moves between us. He wraps his arms around me, trapping mine at my side, an expertly executed, warm comforting bear hug. And slowly, he walks me back:

'Woah ... Joe, Joooe. It's okay, it's over. Let's all just relax mate. No-one's doing any more shouting, okay.'

'You fucking tell him that then. TO KEEP HIS FUCKING MOUTH SHUT. I ain't here to do his dirty work.'

'Okay, okay. I'm sorry.'

With his head now bowed so as to avoid my eyes, the doctor backs away.

'You fucking wanna be mate. I'm telling ya, you shout at me again, AN...'

The calming voice of the ward sister enters my head. She positions herself to break my stare. To bring me down. To slow my thoughts:

'Shushh, it's okay. It's all fine Joe. Let's just calm down. Take a breath. Count to ten, and calm.'

And in my head: - *'One ... Two ... Three ...'* - The kindness in those eyes. Those curves. That hair.

'Now there'll be no more shouting, as It's just upset everyone.'

'Seven ... Eight ...' - And all the way. With each word the anger subsides, and the porter releases his hold, as he knows I am now hers:

'Now you two, go and get a mop, so we can get this mess cleaned up.'

Honestly, this place! It can properly do your head in if you're not careful.

2

If I were to tell you a secret, something I've not told any other human being. Something I've kept real close. Say we were the best of mates. I mean proper tight. Or better still lovers. Yeah, say we were lovers. That secret, would you keep it? Or when the friendship was gone. Say the love had been ripped from your heart. That we had got to the point where you could not bear the sight of this face, or to even hear the sound of me breathing. That secret, would you keep it? Or, if need be. Or worse still, should an opportunity arise. That very same secret, would you use it against me?

3

Let's just make something very clear before we go any further, I'm not asking you to like me. In fact, the more we go on, I'd imagine it to be quite the opposite. Which is fair enough. Each to their own and all that. But you need to understand that I'm not looking for mates. I've got loads of mates, proper mates. The type of mate who'd drop everything to come and help if needed. I don't need or want your approval, your understanding or anything. I require nothing from you. And so, if you want to continue, fine. If not, whatever! And I'm not trying to be arsey, or play the hard man or any of that bullshit, I'm just saying, if you want to stop here, then that's fine by me. I didn't come looking for you, remember. I don't care about you. Why would I, we've never met! If I knew you then things might be different, but I don't. And so why would I care? You mean nothing to me. I think we, *you and I,* we just need to get that straight. I couldn't give a flying fuck about you, your life, or what you think of me. At this point, it's you, you should be thinking about.

4

I remember the warm water flowing down her neck. It crossed her shoulders and caressed the perfect curves of that perfect body. I sensed her warm soapy fingers working between her legs as she pushed back to feel every inch of me inside her. Although to be fair, I was doing my best to give her all of it anyway.

'I'm going to come. Fuck me. Fuck me harder, you dirty boy. Harder ...'

I grabbed her hair and pulled her head back. She liked that. And I felt that mix of pleasure and pain pulse through her:

'Go on, harder. I'm going to come. Give it me. Harder ... harder ...'

And those words, her words, they pushed me over the edge. She reached around and dug her nails deep into me, returning the pleasurable, painful sensation I had offered her, forcing me into one final thrust.

'Don't stop. Fuck me. Don't stop … stay inside me …'

She pushed back, grinding her arse round and round, forcing me backwards. Until I felt her tighten around me, and she held me there. Her pussy pulsing. Her breath, like mine panting. I released her hair, and as she straightened I wrapped my arms around her. And our breathing slowed. And a few relaxing moments passed, before she thrust her arse back, and forced me out. Job done.

'Naughty boy.' She said. 'Now get out.'

I told her I loved her.

'I said, get out. You've had your fun. I need to shower.'

And it's true, I do love her. And if anyone were to lay a finger on her, I swear, I'd kill them. I know a lot of fellas say stuff like that, but seriously, I would. Given the chance, I'd murder the cunt. I'd rip his cock off, and I'd fuck his face with it until he choked to death on his own cum, the dirty fucking weasel, touching my girl like that. I know a lot of fellas boast of such things, but seriously … I'm not like a lot of fellas.

She was also heading away that weekend, a trip with the girls, spa retreat or some such bollocks. I watched as she took underwear from a drawer and placed it in her case. It was the good stuff, expensive.

One set electric blue, the other bright pink. Both sets lacy, sexy, feminine. I loved seeing her in those, and she knew it. She's such a sexy little thing. At the time I couldn't help but think: - *'Bit racy for a girls weekend.'* - And I knew she'd put them there on purpose, for me to see. But it's all part of the game, eh! And we all play it, *the game*. Still, I trust her, I always have. Because without trust you've got nothing. I mean if you can't trust the ones you love, why the fuck would you bother to love them?

5

We left early on the Friday to make the most of the weekend. Myself, Darren, Philbs, Eddy, Keith, Ryan and Iffy. Now there's a reason Iffy's called Iffy.

A good few years back Iffy headed off to Asia in order to *find himself*. Well that's what he told his dear old mum anyway. He'd actually fucked off so that certain other people couldn't find him, if you know what I mean? But mums being mums, well they don't need to hear all that do they? Like a lot of young men on that journey out east, Iffy only made it as far as Bangkok, mainly due to the vast amount of horizontal refreshment that is so readily available in that part of the world to young fuckwits such as himself.

One night while partaking in some oral stimulation, Iffy sat up to reach for a cheeky little stroke of the horse's nose, only to find that the particular filly he was with turned out to be quite a big part donkey! Their eyes locked. They both froze. Until, after a few long moments of not quite knowing what to do, Iffy slowly let go and began to lean back. However, the he/she currently positioned between his legs, and with his cock still in situ', decided to test the water by pushing a digit up Iffys' bum! Now, like most people, Iffy can't resist a bargain and, having paid in advance, well! Best blow job he's ever had apparently! His big mistake was coming back and telling Eddy, because within an hour we all knew. And from that moment on, Christopher J Mills became known as Iffy. Iffy's also the supplier of the Class A's; the pills and the powder that keep weekends such as that jogging along, just the way they are meant to.

I travelled up to Euston with Keith. The station concourse was alive as ever, the usual mix of Saturday morning travellers. Shoppers heading out, tired and wired clubbers heading home. There were the lovers, the lonely, and the lowlife. Those looking for a bag to pick, or a runaway to maybe buy a coffee, befriend, and then ruin. It's all there if you stop to look. If you take the time that is. Keith had nipped off to get a burger, although on the way up he'd told me he'd already eaten, the fat fuck! And so, I made my way to Platform

Fourteen alone. I spotted Eddy first. As always, he stood a few steps away from the others. Funny that, that he always seems to keep some distance. He is a funny one is Eddy. And when I say *funny*, I mean *funny funny*, rather than *funny ha ha*. Fuck knows why he's so moody. Maybe there's something in the past, something he's not shared. Some secret he's locked away. Huh, secrets! A seemingly insignificant sentence thrown his way. Or a moment. But something, trapped deep in his memory. Something he dare not tell. A memory that eats away at him. Those often tiny things that unknowingly shape us. Or maybe not! Maybe there's nothing locked in that head of his. Maybe he was just born a miserable bastard. Either way, he's the easiest bloke in the world to wind up. Eddy could start an argument in a lift on his own. And he won't say three words when two will do:

'Where's Keith?' he asked.

'He's gone for a burger.'

'Fat cunt!'

See!

Unlike Eddy, Darren and Philbs, well, they never stop talking. Yackety fucking yak, all, day, long. Out of all of us I'd say Darren is the sensible one. Apart from me, of course. And when I say sensible, what I mean is that Darren don't just fly off the handle, like Philbs can. That said, Philbs flying off the handle is a beautiful sight. Believe me I know, I've seen it. Because you see the thing with Philbs is, he ain't shy when it comes to punching people. In fact, none of us are. It's probably why we get on so well – our collective liking for violence.

6

All I was doing was sitting there minding my own business, lost in my thoughts. As we all are from time to time. You, me. All lost, from time to time. And to be fair, I had a lot to think about that day. Which was why I was in the boozer in the first place. Inside, rather than out. Because I remember, it was a fucking hot day that was. Which was why the pub was virtually empty. I mean, I imagine most people would have been thinking: - *'What kind of prick would sit inside on a day like this?'* - Well the answer to that is someone with a lot to think about. Someone like me. Because, as I say, I had an awful lot to think about.

And so there I was just sitting there, staring at what was left of my pint, half full. As opposed to half empty. I'm definitely a half full kind of bloke. Well you've got to be ain't ya, what with everything! And his voice, it cut across the room almost as if I were meant to hear it. As if someone, something, other than just him wanted those words to hit home. Thick it was. His accent. Thick. Thick set. Like him. I mean he had to be twenty stone if he was an ounce. The one doing all the talking. The one willing me to hear. A right old lump he was. Him and two others, one half his size, but taller – a proper rake of a fella. The other about five-seven I'd say, about the same as me but fatter, much fatter. I don't know, fifteen stone maybe? I'm what, eleven and a half? Doesn't matter really. And there they were, standing at the bar, the only others like me, inside rather than out. Those three Irish fellas, all on the lager. Which I thought: - *'Strange, them being on the lager, rather than the Guinness.'* - Because you know what they're like, eh, those, *pikeys*. And those words of his, oh they hit home all right:

'So, I said to him, you're two grand short on the money here, it's five grand you're owing me. The quote was for the labour only. The materials was extra. The old cunt, shaking like a fucking leaf he was. His missus threatened to call the police. I said, Go on. Call the fucking police, see if I care! But if you do, I'll nail your fucking dog of yours to the door.'

'And not a pint of Guinness between 'em.' – I thought.

'So did you get the extra money?' asked the Rake.

'Did I fuck! She'd already called the cops. Daft

fucking bitch. But you know the score, they don't want to know. My word against theirs. I left the cunts to it. I'd got me three grand anyways. But I went back all right. I fucking hated that dog. Always sniffing around my feet it was.'

I watched as he downed what was left of his pint, half empty I'd say. He seemed a half empty kind of fella to me, judging by his words:

'I went back. I snapped that yappy little fucker's neck, and I nailed it to the door. What kind of a fucking dog is that anyways?'

I watched as he planted the empty glass down on the bar.

'Right, it's your round. I'm off for a piss.'

And off to the toilet he went, leaving the Rake and Tubby leaning at the bar, their backs to me. I finished my pint. Half full remember? And I gave it a count of: - *One ... two ... three ...* - and all the way up to: - *... ten.* - And then I head off to join him. I entered to see him stood at the urinals, cock in one hand, the other pressed against the wall in order to steady himself. I took position at his side, and staring straight ahead, as men do, I joined the piss party:

'You alright mate?'

He clearly wasn't in the mood for conversation. But I continued, nonetheless.

'I said, are you alright? Are you having a nice day?'

Staring straight ahead, as men do, he reluctantly

offered me a terse reply:

'Yeah, I'm having a great, fucking, day.'

His tone clearly indicated a desire for me to mind my own fucking business, but I was far from done:

'That's nice then eh. You have a great day and all that.'

I slipped my hand into my pocket. The cold sensation of metal on my fingertips brought a wave of pleasure. A wash of joyful calmness. Of relief. And then, staring straight ahead, as men do, I continued:

'You're a big lump eh!'

My words clearly rattled him:

'What did you fucking say?'

'I said, you're a big lump. A FAT CUNT.'

My thumb expertly flicked the blade free. And with the weapon now primed, and ready. And with my eyes fixed firmly on the stained white tiles before me, I pulled the blade from my pocket and, staring straight ahead, as, men, do … for I could not bring myself to look, I sliced down. Blood burst from where piss had just flowed. Deep crimson splattered the porcelain before us, sending it a beautiful wash of red. The lump dropped to the floor, clutching at his severed cock. And his screams they quickly fell silent, as the sight of life draining from him brought a sudden darkness to his world. Shame, because I really wanted him to know why. Surely you understand, right? Or do I have to explain everything?

7

We arrived to find the hotel was run down and dated. But then again, so is Blackpool. That said, the rooms were cheap. As was the clientele. Groups of men and women, away for the weekend. Stags and Hens in fancy dress. Men dressed as superheroes, when in truth they were nothing more than sheep. Women dressed as princesses and fairies, most with wings far too flimsy to lift their heavy frames.

When did that become the norm? Dressing like a cunt to celebrate the love of two friends. Men dressed as superheroes for fuck's sake! Come midnight, most would be committing crimes rather than solving them. Crimes of lust, fuelled by alcohol, Class A's and the opportunity of being away from the ones they say they love. Come morning I dare say some of those princesses would be bowing their heads in shame, as they picked at the *all you can eat* breakfast buffet. Piling eggs, upon bacon, upon half-cooked hash browns, upon the shame they've brought upon themselves. Their tiaras broken. Their children unknowing.

Don't get me wrong, I don't blame them for their behaviour. For all I knew they may be stuck in loveless marriages. Or worse still, with abusive partners where it's easier to stay than it is to leave the mortgage. It's just that! That conveyor belt of shit those people buy into. Shit lives, celebrating shit lives to be. Men and women dressing as children for a bit of organised *fun, fun, fun*. And why, eh? Why? - *'Because it's what everybody else does!'* - WELL FUCK EVERYBODY ELSE! WHY BE WHAT *THEY* WANT? LIVE, LIVE FOR FUCK SAKE. BE YOURSELF! LIVE! Captain, Cunting, America does not live, eat, shit and fuck in Blackpool. He's not even real!

8

When I was a kid, I'd spend most of my summer holidays down the canal with my three best mates, Dave, Keith, a different Keith, mind, and Brian. Now they were truly the best of days. We were so lucky to have each other. Just boys being boys. Growing up and playing up. Jumping rivers, climbing trees and putting coins on the railway tracks for the trains to squash and send whizzing back past our ears. Just the four of us, the best of mates. Brian was a lovely kid. A gentle, kind, funny boy. He was brought up by his nan, who we were always led to believe was his mum. But she weren't. She was his nan.

Then one day Brian was walking across town, through another estate and some lads chased him. Older lads. *Hard lads*. When they were together. They chased Brian up an alley and they beat him up. A proper hiding it was an' all. They broke his leg! That's some hiding that eh, breaking a young boy's leg? I lost one of my best mates that day. Because Brian, well, never came out much after that. I did hear though, that a good few years later, when he got into his late teens, Brian started going out again, only on his own. And he picked those lads off, one, by, one. The hard lads. *When they were together.*

He had those lads looking over their shoulder every time they left the house or the boozer. Who knows, they might still be looking now? Because I tell ya, it never leaves you. Both the fear and the hate. IT NEVER, FUCKING, LEAVES YOU! Who'd have thought it, gentle, kind, funny little Brian, owning, *owning*, those who thought they could so easily own him?

9

Washed and readied we headed out on the town, the cold grey sea to our left, tiny shops and run-down arcades to our right, all desperately clinging on in the hope that it might still just happen. Couples walked hand in hand, some laughing, others deep in conversation. A few no doubt wishing they were somewhere else. Anywhere else. Maybe even with someone else. And on benches and in the doorways sat the drunks and the beggars, their hands held out.

I used to feel sorry for the drunks and the beggars. Used to. But not any more. It's not good enough. It's not good enough to just sit there with your hand out, expecting. This world it does not owe you a living. At least try! Do something! Anything! Draw on the pavement. Buy a tin whistle and blow me a shit tune. But don't just sit there! ...

But how? How can you say such a thing? How can you voice such words? Where's your compassion? Where's your humanity? Some of those poor people will have ended up there beaten, abused and unwanted and ...' - Yeah, yeah. Blah, blah fucking blah. I know that. I understand all of that.

But you know what? The beaten, the abused and unwanted, they walk amongst us all day long. They stand next to us in queues. They stack shelves in supermarkets. They drive our trains, and they teach our children. They don't just sit with their hands out. They get on with it. Survivors. Each and every one of them, a survivor. They get, the fuck, on with it! And so no. No sympathy for the drunks and the beggars. Because at least on top of all that all they have is nothing! No debt, no bills, no responsibility. Imagine that. Imagine the freedom that would bring? And yet they want my hard-earned money! And for what? So that they can go do what I've slogged all week to go and do? To go and get wasted, so that I, for a few short hours can forget about the weights they don't even carry? Well fuck that! If they want it, earn it! Go on, dance for me. Dance. Just as I am forced to dance.

10

I fucked her in the toilet, trap Five. Lines chopped, scraped, shaped and snorted to the back of the neck. In the background chains flushed away imaginary pill shits. Piss bounced off metal urinals. Lads wished friends, and strangers well. And all along there she was, that girl from the Valleys, bent over, arse in the air, hands clutching at the cistern. And in and out, and in and out I went, and she pushed back. She was a bit of a unit if truth be told, but I don't mind that, a bit of meat. I remember she had a pretty face. And she made me laugh at the bar. But d'ya know what really reeled me in? What really sealed the deal? It was the accent. Ohhh, that accent. It must have melted a million hearts and mine besides. It's just, beautiful. Almost magical. Lyrical. Like poetry and birdsong mixed into one:

'Go on, fuck me. Fuck me harder you English bastard!'

'A tad jingoistic.' - I thought. But I liked it, as in and out I went, and she pushed back. In truth it could have been anyone. As could I of course! For she was clearly using me as much as I her. I had a flashback to me and mine in the shower that very morning. She'd have gone mental if she could have seen me. And rightly so. And I dare say that one bent over, arse in the air, hands clutching at the cistern, had a fella back in the valleys, who, if he would have seen her, if he could have seen us, would have snapped our necks there and then. Just as I would have done if I'd have caught some weasel little cunt, clattering into the back of my, beautiful, girl. But hey, as I said, it could have been anyone. It didn't mean anything. It was just a fuck!

Huh! The lame excuses we try to give ourselves. Such weakness. Such wasted pointless words. *It didn't mean anything?* Oh, it meant EVERYTHING! *It was just a fuck!* Such misplacing of trust. Such destroying of love. I should be ashamed. I am ashamed. Such moments should have me bowing my head in utter, utter disgrace. I never once said I was any better than those back at the hotel, Okay? Never once did I say such words. That said, at least that one bent over and I, weren't dressed as Scoobie fucking Doo and Wonder Woman. We clearly both had standards:

'Go on fuck me! Fuck me harder! But don't cum in

me, cum on my arse. I've got some wet-wipes in my bag!'

See, standards! Five minutes later I was back at the bar at Ryan's side.

'Where the fuck have you been?'

'In the bog. Having a shit.'

As I said, it could have been anyone.

11

On those summer holidays when I'd go down the canal with my three best mates, Dave, Keith, a different Keith mind, and Brian. Every now and again there'd be two other lads from school down there, Kev and Wayne. Wayne! Who the fuck calls their kid Wayne? Even back then it was a cunt's name! Kev and Wayne just loved to shoot stuff; birds, water rats. They'd even shoot the fish if they were sat up top of the water on hot days trying to breathe. I mean, you could be in mid conversation with them, talking about girls, football, the tele, and they'd see something, stop, aim, shoot, and kill it, and then just carry on talking as though nothing had happened. Just the pointless ending of life. They didn't even seem to get that much enjoyment out of it. I think they'd killed so much that the novelty had just worn off. I fucking hated them. Particularly Wayne, spindly little prick.

Then one day they were down there shooting squirrels. I mean, baby squirrels, for fuck's sake! And that was it, I flipped. I'd seen enough. And I went, and I got right in Wayne's face. And you have to believe me, as true as these words are spilling from my lips, you have to believe me, I was right up in his face. I swear I was. And I told him. I told him what a fucking coward he was, shooting poor, defenceless little animals like that. And that if he had anything about him, he'd pick on something that could fight back. Oh and I'd happily fight him. And you have to believe me, I was right in his face. I swear, I was right up in his fucking face. And I grabbed that pistol from his hand. And I placed it to my side. And I swear, I swear, I didn't even look. I just wanted to unload the fucking thing. I wasn't even looking. And I pulled that trigger ... BANG ... And a cheer went up. And I looked around to see, that I'd hit a duck right in the fucking neck. Its head lolloped forward and fell under the water. And its wings, they started flapping. And it went round and round in circles. And as they stood there laughing, all I could do was watch as this other duck, its partner. Because ducks do that, they partner up for life, I'm sure they do. Someone told me that, I'm sure they did. At least I think so?

This other duck, its partner, it flew down and did all it could to lift its head above water, to keep it breathing, to keep it alive. But it just kept lolloping back under over, and over, and over. Until the flapping stopped. And the thing fell still.

When I got home that night, I went to my bed, I pulled the covers over my head, and I cried. I cried like I'd never cried before and I have never cried since. If I could change one thing. If I could go back to just one moment of my time on this earth, then I swear it would be that. And I'd go back. And I'd get right in that spindly little prick Wayne's face. And I'd tell him what a fucking coward he was. I'd grab that pistol from his hand, and I swear. I swear, as true as these word spill from deep within me, I SWEAR ... I'd blow my fucking brains out. Just to end the guilt I have carried from that moment on.

12

We left the club at 2:00am and headed to The Marmaris takeaway. Marmaris, Maramis, or whatever the fuck it was called. It was Turkish or Greek owned. Again, I don't know. I don't care. D'you know what, I don't even know why I mention it. We'd gone there so that Philbs could stuff that big fat belly of his. Do you ever stop to wonder what it must be like for the poor bastards on the other side of those counters, that time of the night, early morning, sober, looking on at the likes of us, the end of the night dregs? That place, The Marmaris, Maramis, whatever the fuck it was. That place was someone's dream for fuck's sake! How those dreams must have turned once the boat docked and the penny dropped ...

'Fuck this place. Fuck England and all that sail in her.

Come midnight these drunken ferrets just can't help themselves. Let's just get our heads down and fill their fat pasty white bellies. Ten years! Ten years hard graft, just ten years, and then my love I promise, I swear we'll return. We'll return to the crystal-clear waters of home. Where we will live like Sultans. And our children will bathe alongside the sun-kissed bodies of Gods and Goddesses, rather than dodging the used Durex and empty bottles that bob around this windy little shit hole on the edge of Europe. Ten years. Ten years hard work, and then my love, I promise. I swear, we will return.'

Ten years! Ten long years! That's no dream. For in that time you're going to encounter a whole bunch of wankers:

'Oh for fuck's sake mate, you've put red cabbage on here! I said no red cabbage. What part of that d'ya not fucking get?'

His words lifted my head just in time to see him chuck the offensive belly filler back on the counter. And on seeing a chance to jump the queue, Philbs moved in:

''Ere mate, I'll have that if he don't want it.'

'Just fucking hold on will ya. Get back in fucking queue and let him sort me out, for fuck sake!'

'Alright mate. You wanna calm down.'

Now in fairness to Philbs I do clearly remember him asking, well telling, the fella to calm down. I do clearly remember that:

'Yeah Philbs mate, get back here and let the fella get sorted for Christ's sake.' shouted Darren.

I told ya, he's sharp is Darren. He can smell trouble:

'Yeah, do as your pal says and get back in the fucking queue.'

But by now Philbs was not for listening. He turned to the man behind the counter:

'Don't worry about him mate, just give us that 'ere.'

'Listen pal, just do as your mate says and get back in the queue will ya? Because you know what, you're really starting to get on my fucking tits here!'

'Well get your tits out of my face and we won't have a problem, will we son?'

'Problem? You want a problem I'll give you a fucking prob...'

And there you go. Fucking ridiculous. Those dreams so easily turned. And all over a bit of red cabbage! Philbs spun on his heels and planted a right hander straight into cabbage boy's face. The lad staggered back, his nose broken, his shirt splattered claret. And then, already out cold, he fell between two tables, before coming laid to rest alongside the squashed chips and limp lettuce that graced the floor of someone's dream:

'ONE PUNCH? ONE FUCKING PUNCH, YOU TRAPPY LITTE CUNT,' screamed Philbs.

A hunger for violence clearly having overtaken that within his belly:

'Oh for fuck's sake Philbs! Let's get out of here before the Old Bill turn up.'

'FUCK THE OLD BILL!'

Like I say, dreams so easily turned. That said, and I do have to hold my hands up here, for I do remember thinking at the time, as indeed I still do, that: *'I am actually with Philbs on the red cabbage.'* - I mean: - *'What's the fella's problem with red cabbage?'* - I remember thinking: - *'Personally I love the stuff. It's lovely, raw, in a kebab.'* - I thought: – *'Or better still brazed with caramelised onions in a nice thick gravy. Poured over roast spuds. Proper roast spuds mind, crispy on the outside, soft in the middle.'* - My head, from here to there. From this to that: - *'How Philbs could have even thought of eating after all that gear he'd had! Fuck knows how fat he'd be if he didn't whack so much gak up his nose! But still, the lad didn't deserve that. Not over a bit of red cabbage. I've got a mate that don't like cheese! How the flying fuck can you not like cheese? Still, it doesn't mean he deserves knocking out over it, does it! It's just a bit of fucking cheese!'* - I thought: - *'Oh, I do love a good bit of cheese. In a sandwich. Fresh crusty white bread, loads of butter, a big slab of cheese, raw onion, some salad cream. And yeah, while we're at it why not, some freshly cut raw, red, cabbage.'* - I remember thinking, amongst all that. And all along, there was that poor bastard, just lying there. All limp. Like the lettuce.

13

The walk back to the hotel seemed to take longer for some reason, I don't know why. Cars passed, music blaring. The odd shout of drunken camaraderie was offered up from passenger windows: *'Oi, Oiii!'* ... Along with the odd insult of course: *'Waaaaankers.'* ... Well, this is England after all! Two lads stood, hands in pockets as a third, their mate, pissed between two cars. Me? I was head down, lost in my thoughts. If I remember rightly, I was thinking about cheese.

A flash of pure white caught my eye. A cat had darted from a garden path. It stopped, as did I. And I couched, and I watched, as it looked back over its shoulder for a count of: - *One ... two ... three ... four ... five ...* - Then a noise – *snap* - sent it bolting out into the road. I lifted. The car.

Gun metal grey. The driver, male. The passenger, female. A split second. That flash of pure white. Gun metal grey. The driver. An Audi. A passenger. The sudden screeching of brakes. The look of horror on her face. And then, *doof*. A low, dull, sickening thud. Then, *Doof*, another. Her inaudible scream as they passed. The burning stench of rubber staining my nostrils. All of it jumbled up. A brief, tiny moment of my time on this earth, but now forever locked in. Bad that. Really bad.

I headed out into the road and there it was, its head moulded to the tarmac, a yellowy red mush against the pure angelic white of its body. A body that flapped around like a bin liner in the wind. Its legs still running, desperate to escape its fate, its pain, its end. But there was of course no escape.

Why? Why did I have to see that, eh? *Why?* Why put me through that? What lesson was I to learn from such a pointless ending of life? WHY? Those fucking Gods of yours! They don't half move in mysterious ways. I tried not to look, but in truth I could not help myself. And I began to pace in circles. Round and round I went, my mind on fire. The pain and the anger raging deep inside of me:

'Fucking hell. Loooook. Look at the state of the fucking thing. Eddy mate! Look at it. It's still trying to run, for fuck's sake!'

'Jesus, look at the state of its head!' said Darren.

I'm sure it was Darren. And round and round I went:

'Eddy mate loooook, look at it. It's still trying to fucking run.'

And with that Eddy stepped forward and brought his boot down hard on what was left of its head ... once ... twice ... and then a third time, so as to put the poor thing, to put us both, out of our misery. And still I tried not to look, but my eyes, they just would not let me. And round and around I paced. And I couldn't help but think: - *'How much I like cats. Of how I really like cats. Of how I prefer them to dogs. Not that I'm having a go.'* - I thought: – *'I mean I like dogs. Dogs are lovely. They're friendly, sociable animals, unlike cats. And obviously they say a dog is a man's best friend! Well they say that. My best friend is Dave.'* - As I've already mentioned: – '*Dave from over the road. Not that he lives there now, of course.'* - I remember thinking: - *'And one of the reasons Dave's my best friend is that whenever I've gone for a walk with Dave, he's never suddenly stopped and asked me to pick a turd up in a Tesco carrier bag! So I'll take my chances with Dave on the old walking front.'* - I thought: - *'Not that Dave has ever shat himself in the street!'* – My mind from here to there: - *'Not to my knowledge anyway. And I'm sure he'd have told me if he had, what with him being such a good mate and all that. It's just that I prefer cats. You see cats, well they ain't like dogs, are they? A dog is all fetch this, fetch that. Dogs do as they're told. They might as well be one of us! So easily tricked. So easily led. So quick to follow. Whereas a cat, well, he'll tell you to fetch your own fucking stick. And by the way, here's my arsehole while you're at it!'* - And seeing the state of that poor thing, well. And round and around I went, thinking: - *'No-one was to blame. Who knows why the thing bolted? Who knows what it was running from? Five seconds either side and we'd have all been on our way none the wiser.'* – I thought.

But something made it run. Something brought it to its end. And I lifted my eyes from the tarmac to see that the car, they'd just driven off: – *'Such cowards.'* - And slowly my pacing dropped. Though my head continued to spin a million spins. And I took a seat at the kerb. And I placed my head in my hands. And my stomach held such a pain, both twisted and knotted. Though there were no tears. Because I knew that no-one was to blame this time: - *'Certainly not myself.'* – I thought: - *'Five seconds either side, all none the wiser.'* - Eddy came to sit at my side. And then he told the others:

'You lot head back, we'll follow when he's ready.'

Strange how what appears to be the smallest of things to some, can mean so much to others. To Philbs, Darren and the rest, it was just a cat: *'It's just a fucking cat mate, get over yourself'*, they'd say. But it wasn't. It was so much more. It was a life so pointlessly taken. Snuffed out, extinguished. And the very next day someone would be out searching. Pictures would be pinned to trees, or attached to lamp posts. A name would be called, hopeful, but in vain. Someone would be shedding tears, maybe some kids, a young couple, or an old lady, her one companion, the one thing that keeps her loneliness at arm's length, now gone. The harsh reality of knowing that it can all end, just like that. Out of all of them I think only Eddy understands. At least I think he does! Please, let that be true, I couldn't bear the thought that it was just me.

14

There was no hurry in getting back, as the drugs we'd taken kept sleep at bay. And as Eddy and I walked, I asked him:

'If you had one wish, just one wish, and you could do anything, what would you do?'

'I'd travel. I'd leave these shitty little towns behind, and I'd travel the world.'

And Eddy told me that he'd once read this book: *The Blue Road*, by some fella called *Windy* something, who'd joined the merchant navy as a young lad because, well let's just say Iffy wasn't the only one who needed to get away. *Windy Baboulene*, that was it. *Windy Baboulene* was his name. Now that's some name, eh! And Eddy told of how this lad had travelled the world on a container ship, and the older fellas, the seasoned sailors, they made his life hell, because he was new to the game. They constantly wound him up and played jokes on him. Because that's what they did to first timers. It was something all the seasoned sailors had been through themselves. A kind of initiation every sailor had to endure on their first circumnavigation of the planet.

But it wasn't vicious or nasty, it was just fun. Their way of killing the loneliness of the oceans. Well, fun for the old timers anyway. In truth they all had his back, just as they had each other's. And he told of how every port had its own story. And being sailors, they knew all the best, and worst places to go. Oh, and the stories this lad told! Huh.

'What a thing to do.' said Eddy.

And yes, what a thing to do! To travel the world like that, as a lad. That lad, who talked of seeing the stars, how he could never have ever imagined them. Of the vastness of the sea, the sense of isolation it brought, and the power it held.

And that book, it had struck a chord with Eddy, or so he said. And it had made him wonder about his place in this world. And of how the seas must make you realise just how small and unimportant you are. And he'd imagine being in the middle of nowhere, hundreds of miles from anyone. Isolated with no-one to bail him out. Just himself and his fellow seamen alone and at the mercy of the ocean. And how he felt it would be good for the soul. That it would make him realise just how lucky he was to be alive. And so I asked him:

'Then why not go?'

And he didn't really know what had, or continued to hold him back. Or have the answer to what stops any of us doing the things we dream of doing, other than fear. Fear of the unknown. The same fear that makes us settle. And then he asked me:

'And what about you? If you had one wish, what would you do?'

I knew the answer. But I didn't feel the need to share. Up ahead a fox appeared. And it bounced on its paws as it hugged the bushes.

'Tch, tch, tch.'

It stopped. And just as the cat had done, it looked back over its shoulder. And its eyes they fixed upon us, just as ours did upon him. And a few seconds passed. And then it was gone.

'Ain't they just the most beautiful creatures, Eddy?'

But by now Eddy had drifted. His mind, oceans away.

15

We left early the next morning, and caught the ten twenty one to Preston. Early, considering the previous night's excesses. Once there, we crossed platforms to catch a train to Wigan. As ever our eyes were on the lookout for like-minded souls. A few were spotted - they usually are on such mornings - but the day was young, and time was short. For a Saturday the carriage was surprisingly empty, and so we took the tables closest to the doors. As I remember, it was just as Ryan headed off for a piss that we first spotted him, the young lad, the Down's Syndrome kiddie.

'Fucking hell! What's this cunt come as?' said Philbs.

I think it was Philbs.

For there he was, heading our way, dressed from

head to toe in Spiderman gear. Cap back to front, like a cunt. Hoody, rucksack, the lot. And as Ryan passed, well he just couldn't help himself:

'Alright Batman, how's it going?'

Spidey stopped:

'I'm not Batman. My name is Alan.'

The lads cracked up. But not me. And once at our side Spidey stopped and spoke to Darren. And with not a care in the world:

'Excuse me, but can I sit there please?'

He pointed to the seat by the window, the seat Ryan had just left. And Darren, he laughed, well you would, wouldn't you? But not at young Spidey of course, you do understand that, right?:

'No, you can't. Go and sit somewhere else. Go on, there are loads of empty seats.'

'But I want to sit there.'

'Well you can't, my mate's sitting there. Now go on, jog on.'

'No he isn't, it's empty. Don't be horrible.'

And the lads, they laughed even more. For now there was fun to be had. But again, not at Spidey's expense. You do understand that? And the lads, they chipped in, even me:

'Yeah, don't be horrible'

'Horrible Darren. Let him sit down.'

'Yeah he's right. No one's sitting there.'

'Ycah, lct him in you prick.'

'Horrible Darren.'

And so Darren, he gave in:

'Oh for fuck's sake! Go on then.'

He lifted from his seat and let young Spidey in. But instead of taking the window, Spidey, well he took the aisle, leaving Darren standing like a plumb. And fuck me, did we laugh:

'Oh mate, he's proper cunted you off there Dazzer. Proper cunted you off!' said Keith.

At least I think it was Keith.

Darren used his hip to try and barge the youngster over, but he was not for moving. They're quite solid, those Down's kids:

'Oi shift over.'

'No. Not going to.'

And we laughed. And then Ryan returned, freshly powdered:

'Got a new boyfriend have ya Dazzer? 'Ere, shift over will ya mate?'

And with that Spidey did shift. And he took the window:

'Ha. He's done you again Daz. Properly mugged you off. You should try being nicer, mate. Horrible Darren.' said Philbs at Darren's second *cunting* ...

And it was definitely Philbs, that said that. Then Ryan asked the lad:

'So, where you off to then?'

'I'm going to meet my auntie. We're going shopping.'

'Off to buy some Batman gear are ya?'

And at that, Spidey looked puzzled:

'No! Why do you keep talking about Batman? You're stupid.'

And we laughed. But not at him. And by now I really do hope that you've got your head around that. But laugh we did, as he sat there with his hands on his knees. And that Down's kiddie, he eyed us all up. What a fucking legend, for he had not a care, or a fear in the world. Not that he realised it, of course. For if he had, if he had been a *normal* lad, taking the piss the way he had, or talking to us as he had done, well, we'd have ripped him a new arsehole. But no, not a care, or a fear. For he was far from *normal*. Whatever *normal* means. Maybe *normal* is the wrong choice of word. But he was certainly different. And it's a bloody good job that he was! Though again, I dare say some would take offence at the use of such a statement.

Even though he was, clearly, very different from Darren, Iffy or I. Young Spidey, well he was clearly chalk and cheese to any of us. That doesn't mean he was any less of a man. In fact, I'd imagine him to be a far better man than I will ever be, if indeed he were to make it that far, because well, those Down's kids, they don't all last that long now do they! Though better he most probably was. For I very much doubt he'd ever set out on a Saturday with the intent I had resting inside of me. And yet some will take offence at such words, for we must now treat all as one, as equals, the same. Though some clearly need more care, and more love. And some, some like Spidey, well they have more love to give. For Spidey's kind, well they do love a cuddle, eh! And let's face it, who doesn't like a cuddle? – *Are you alright there Susie?* - And yet you want him to be loved, and to be looked after, and treated as I should be? Such hypocrites.

As if I deserve such kindness. As if I deserve such love. So be thankful. Be thankful that I, that we, my friends and I, that we see through your words. For your words and your gestures are nothing but gifts to yourself. So, as I say, be thankful it was us he fell upon, because there are some proper cunts out there. Not all men or boys are equal. We are all far from the same, and with different hands we are dealt. So don't you dare patronise Spidey, or I for that matter. For Spidey and I, we are very different. For he had not a care in this world, as off out shopping with his auntie he headed. Oh to be so innocent, either in this life, or the next. If indeed any of us are offered such an opportunity!

16

When I was a kid, proper small like, I used to have these little people in my head, *The Egg Men*. They weren't little eggs with faces drawn on them, that would have been stupid. They were proper little men, with arms and legs, and everything. And they travelled around in these little silver spaceships of theirs. And at night before I went to sleep The Egg Men and I, we'd sit or I'd lie on my bed and we'd talk about all the bad stuff we'd seen on the television. And then, just before I nodded off, I'd send them out into the night to try and make things better. And those little men, The Egg Men, they were as real to me as I were to them. And I'd often see them in my dreams flying all over the world in those spaceships of theirs, putting things right, and doing all good things we'd talked about. And that, well, it made us all feel better about this ugly world we'd somehow found ourselves in.

Obviously I didn't tell anyone. We kept ourselves to ourselves, The Egg Men and I. Because we didn't want anyone thinking I was mad, or stupid, or anything like that. Although how could I have been? I was a child! And when I think about it now, that's the saddest thing about it. Because when you're a child, well you see straight through it all don't you? As a child you look at the world, at all the misery, the suffering, war and injustice, and you think: - *'Why? Why do we live this way? Why do we do such things to one another, instead of just, living?'* - And you find yourself trailing around the supermarket pulling at your mother's skirt thinking: - *'Why don't we just share what we have here with those who have nothing?'* - And it all seems so simple when you're a child: – *'Why not just, share? Share everything. End the suffering and live as equals?'* - And it all seems so, obvious, when you are, innocent.

And then you arrive at that horrendous day when you suddenly realise that some people don't want the pain to end. That some *thrive* off the suffering of others. And you realise that where there's misery and war, there's also money and power to be gained. And that the ones with the money and the power are the very same people that could put an end to it all, but they don't want to. And the belief hits you, that you, tiny little you, that child, well, you are powerless. And at that very moment, a tiny little piece of you dies. Because the first of their claws has dug itself into you. And without even realising it you, like all those you see around you, in that moment of weakness, you begin to settle. Settle for what you have. For although you care, you care just a little bit less than the moment before. Because they have made you believe you are small. That you are powerless. That you are, nothing.

And it was at that point in my life that the first of those Egg Men began to leave. For they could see that I, just like everyone else, was becoming lost. And my days, they passed. And one by one The Egg Men, they left. And this world, this life, it slowly eats its way inside of you. And even though you know it's all so unfair, all you ever do from that moment on is ask yourself: - '*What can I do*?' - Until you've had asked yourself that question so many times, it becames your justification. And at times I'd find myself sleepwalking through life, while all along thinking what a nice, decent person I am. Until instead of settling for what I had, I, like everyone else, suddenly found myself wanting more, more than the person next to me. And although I still cared, well I think I did - *I do*? - I cared nowhere near as much as I should, despite it all staring me in the face, day in day out. Until eventually you realise that well, you've just become the next cunt in the queue. And the last of those Egg Men, those beautiful little men in their spaceships who knew so much, they had no choice but to desert me, just as I had deserted them. If only I had remained loyal, and The Egg Men would have won.

Instead of *Them*.

17

At Wigan we hooked up with those travelling up for the day. Those men we joined, they owned that carriage. Handshakes were made, friendships rekindled, jokes and stories shared. And there we were, all part of it. But not all men, not all boys were welcomed as we were welcomed. A cheer went up at the far end of the carriage. Three lads had entered, young lads in baseball caps and designer gear. It was the uniform that gave them away, because most of the men they had mistakenly fallen upon had, at some time, worn something very similar. Indeed, some still do. However, it was clear from certain parts of their attire that those lads held in their hearts a different love to ours.

Those lads, those three, not-so-innocent lads, and it's important you remember that. Who up until that point had probably strutted that train, staring out the boys, eyeing up the girls! And suddenly here they were, wrong place, wrong time. And there was of course no turning back. Those lads. Those three lads, whose mothers love them no doubt. Whose mothers would have had no idea of the mischief they were hoping to get up to that day. Oh, what kings, what kings they would be if only they could make it through that carriage. What kings! And how they would tell their story, with their heads held high, and their chests pumped out. And no doubt they'd embellish their tale over pints, and on long journeys. Oh, and how they would tell of the day they fronted out those southern pricks with their cocky swagger and their *Oi Oi's!* ... What kings. What kings they would be! If only they could make it through.

With each step, their journey was made harder. Ankles clipped. Shirt sleeves pulled. A baseball cap flicked. Those lads, whose mothers love them lest, we, forget. What kings. What kings they would be, if only they could make those last, few, steps. But let's be honest, that was never going to happen now was it? It was Darren who blocked their path:

'Hello boys. Where you off to?'

The lad out front kept his head bowed. His voice quiet, sheepish even. And I watched as he swallowed hard, desperate to keep the tremble in his voice from showing. But tremble it did, as he bleated his reply:

'We're just off to buffet car.'

'No son, I meant, where you off to today? *After* the buffet car?'

And that lad he pleaded:

'Can we just get round?'

'Aww mate. Don't be going already. We've only just met.'

And with the smell of a kill in his nostrils Darren began to play:

'So, what's your name then, eh?'

'Darren. My name's Darren. Look, can I just please get …'

And Darren, my Darren, he grabbed at the gift:

'No way! My name's Darren too! That's nice ain't it? Me and you both being called Darren. That's nice that, ain't it?'

And the lad, he nodded, though he dare not speak. And as he tried to step past Darren stood firm:

'So, like I said, where are you and your little mates off to today then Darren, *after* you've been to the buffet car? Are you going to football? Because you're dressed like you're going to football. Seriously, in those clothes you look like proper little football fans you do. All done up for the day.'

And I watched as the fear took hold of all three.

'They're just clothes mate. We're not going to football, honest! Are we lads?'

And his friends they joined in:

‘No, no we’re not. We’re just going shopping.’

And a smile came to Darren’s face:

‘Shopping! Really? On a Saturday? Dressed like that?’

‘Yeah, shopping. We don’t like football.’

‘What do you mean, you don’t like football?’ asked Darren, all heads now turned their way:

‘No. We follow rugby. Rugby League,’ said one of the others, desperately searching for a way out. And Darren, my Darren continued:

‘Rugby? Oh right, fair enough. It’s popular up here ain’t it? Rugby? Rugby League?’

And those three lads. Whose mothers love them, no doubt. Those lads who would be kings, they nodded as one. Pleading. Hoping. But Darren wasn’t done:

‘You’re not lying to me are ya? About the rugby? Because you reaaaaally look like proper little football fans to me. Judging by the way you’re dressed and that.’

And those lads, those three not-so-innocent lads, remember, they pleaded:

‘No, we’re not lying. Honest, eh lads? We like Rugby. Wigan.’

And then Philbs joined the chase:

‘Rugby’s gay. All those men grabbing each other’s bollocks in the scrum, that’s gay that is. Is that why you like it? Because you’re gay?’

'No, we're not gay. It's just a good game. Look mate, please can we just ge'....'

But Darren, my Darren, he wasn't for moving. And you could see the fear take hold. And our eyes they fixed upon them:

'Do you like gays?' he asked.

'No. Can we pl ...'

And Darren, he cut him short:

'You don't like gays! Well that's not very nice is it! What's wrong with being gay?'

And he pointed at Iffy:

'See him over there. He got sucked off by a ladyboy. That's pretty gay, ain't it?'

And the men in that carriage, they all cracked up. And a smile came to my face, for I knew the end was near. And young Darren, the other Darren and his mates they laughed too, desperately looking for something, anything to set them free. And he replied:

'Yeah, that's gay.'

And then my Darren, his tone changed:

'You what? Here Iffy, this lad just called you gay mate!'

And Iffy's face, it took a different shine. And the carriage fell silent. And those lads, those lads who would be kings, their laughter died too. As did all hope:

'You've got a fucking nerve ain't ya! Coming in here and calling my mate gay!'

And Darren, my Darren, he lent in. And he lifted the collar on that young lads jacket. And there it was, an enamel badge in the red and white colours of those we'd come to visit. And my smile, it widened, as did Darren's, my beautiful Darren. For the chase had come to an end:

'Oh dear! Looks like someone's been telling me porkies.'

Within seconds, clothes were ripped from backs. Trainers removed. One filled with beer, one with piss, one thrown from the train. Well who needs two trainers? What fun! What fun, we had with those three not-so-innocent lads.

But why? Why would you do such a thing? What is wrong with you? You're a grown man! An adult! Why humiliate those lads so? Lads young enough to be your sons. Why?

How dare you! How *dare* you feel sorry for them! Do you not see? At that moment we gave them a gift. We ignited a fire within their bellies they could never, not in their wildest dreams, ever imagine existed. For at that moment we gave them the burning gift of anger, an anger that will forever rage in their pasty tummies.

Oh, those moments will twist and torment their souls until their dying day. From that moment on their blood will boil at the mere mention of our name. They will spit bile at the sound of our accent. Oh, make no mistake, they will seek revenge for those moments.

And believe me nothing, *nothing* brings with it a sweeter satisfaction than that of violent revenge my friend. And when that moment comes, those lads, those three not-so-innocent lads, and it is so important that you remember and understand that. Those lads, whose mothers love them, I do not fucking doubt! They will look to the heavens, and they will thank us. They will thank us for the gift we gave them that day. Because at that moment they became exactly who they wanted to be ... They became us! ... And so we live on.

18

The police marched us from the platform, up the ramp and out onto the main drag. That beautiful moment of arrival. Us strangers in a distant land. Our heads held high, our arms out wide, and not giving a fuck:

'YELLOW ... YELLOW ... YELLOW ...'

For there we were, in the north ... Huh, the north! The glorious north, my friend. A land of great and proud people, salt of the earth. The kind who bear the weight of this nation - as they do all nations. My brothers, my sisters. Us fleshy little cogs. But on such days we do become enemies. Even though their town is now just the same as my town. The same as every other town. From Workington to Dover, Redcar to Camborne. The same shops, the same burger bars, the same sofa sale that never, fucking, ends! How? How did we allow this to happen? The auctioning off behind our backs of the very things that set us apart. The things of which we should be proud. On which we should build. Of our identity! Slowly but surely they, *THEY*, have moulded and manipulated us all into one, to ensure that the chained now line the pockets of the chains, rather than the local butcher, the baker, or the great men and women who once said, *I can get you that later,* on which these glorious towns and cities of ours were built. Those people I had come to visit deserve better. We all deserve better. You think this game we play is futile. But maybe this is the very reason it is so important to us. Me, my friends and I, and those we had particularly come to visit, we are not so easily sold.

Now eighty strong the police struggled to keep us contained. And as we spread across the road, and we pushed and we shoved, shoppers stopped and gawped. Old women, their trollies packed full of market stall veg, vacuum-packed meat and cheap toilet rolls looked on in awe. Us intruders, a brief moment of excitement to lighten the otherwise dull routine of their diminishing days. Something for them to talk about with others in the pub, or down the club. Or to run past the cat while at home, alone. More often than not, deserted.

A man stared out from a burger bar window. Sat opposite was his child, eagerly colouring in the smiling face of the food chain that kept them warm. A carefully marketed freebie to be imprinted on the child's mind. The unrelenting sell, sell, selling of the brand, of the food, and of the fun to be had. And there they sat, the Saturday afternoon dad and his daughter, killing a few hours until her sixteenth sets them free. Though they will of course never be free.

Obviously he loves her, that goes without saying. Though it has to be said every now and again, just to reassure both her, and himself. That child sat opposite is the most important thing in his life. The one person he'd do anything for. Anything apart from stay with the mother of course, I mean, there's important and there's *important*, right! And so there they sat. And you know what, he's probably glad of the freebie, and the cheap food on offer. Because I dare say money is tight. Probably has been since the day he left. Or, should I say, the day he got caught out. Or she did for that matter. Because we all like a bit of the old in-and-out don't we, both the boys and the girls? And so let's not be too hasty, eh! For it could just as easily have been her, that fucked him over. Though it was probably him. Just saying.

Either way she'll have all the power. They usually get the power, the fairer sex. Even if it were her, that fucked him over. The car, the house, the control, control, controlling. Oh, don't we all just love a bit of control, should the opportunity arise! Still, at least he was free to stare through that burger bar window.

Because elsewhere in that town, as in other towns on such afternoons, there will be men sat in church halls. Men sat opposite their children. Men being watched. Men being judged. Being scrutinised. Men accused of the most horrific acts of abuse against the child they are sat opposite, a slap here, or God forbid, a touch there. If you believe in God, that is? Sick, twisted, abusive men. Is there anything more evil a man can do than to abuse his child? And so there some men sit. Because if there were to be ten men in that hall, if there were fifteen, or twenty even, then statistically, well! And so which one of them is it? Or maybe there are two, or even three, God forbid. If indeed you believe?

And with odds such as that, well, those accusations they simply cannot be ignored. For to abuse a child is the most evil of things - Oh, and the scars that leaves. And so there some evil, twisted, perverted fucking men quite rightly sit.

But equally let's not totally kid ourselves, eh? For within those church halls there will also be some, and I do say *some*. And it is so important that you begin to understand that *some*, men, who have fallen victims themselves. Just has become the child they are sat opposite. Victims of such accusations. Even though those accusing know them not to be true. Accusations that simply can't, and must never be ignored remember, and are therefore so easily placed - Controlling, controlling, controlling. Accusations placed upon them by a woman scorned. Because it's usually the men doing all the scorning of course. But not always, let's not forget! Even though those accusers know, *KNOW* them not to be true!

Can there be a more vile lie placed upon a man's shoulders than such a false accusation against his son, his daughter? And so I wonder, I wonder if those men and women caught up in what was once so precious, but now so, destroyed. If, given the opportunity, they wouldn't return to that special, special night. And at that moment of pure unbridled lust, both prefer that he just pulled out and came on her tits. Or better still, kept his cock to himself, gone home and just knocked himself one out, before falling asleep surrounded by tissue soaked in what might have been. Fuck me, can we turn on the ones we once loved? And yet you judge me for the games I play? Oh, there were far worse than I walking those streets that day. The difference is that me, my friends and I, and those we had particularly come to visit, we are not living a lie. We know exactly who and what we are. And we are not for hiding.

The police pushed us on, and their blue flashing lights silently strobed against the greyness of that place. Their horses strolled at our side. Dogs pulled at leads. Officers on foot eyed us up and down. In the distance a roar went up, and our heads they lifted. Police turned inwards and linked arms. Scarves were pulled over faces. Baseball caps tugged down. Collars turned up. And up ahead the locals stood guard outside their home. That was the moment they'd been waiting for, as had we. That moment when our eyes first met. And their battle cry was sent up to greet us:

'RED ARMY … RED ARMY …'

Adrenalin flowed through my veins, just as it always does at such precious moments. Around me men bounced on their toes, their arms out wide, and an atmosphere of unfolding hatred filled the air. Oh, how I love such moments. Oh, how I love that feeling. That electrifying sensation, the rage welling up inside of me. That burning desire to just let go. And make no mistake, those people opposite, those that called us on, they felt exactly the same. And I love them for it. For without them, I would be empty.

The police penned us against a metal fence. And they held us there. As I am sure they would have done many others over the years. For those little piggies, they do as they do. For they play the game, just as we play. Oh, and my heart it raced. And my blood it pumped. Surely you must wonder? To be the target of such hostility, such hate, such violence? To be there. To be right in amongst it. It must have crossed your mind? And if it has, well, maybe we are not so different after all. Across the road there were plenty of chancers within their ranks. Their feet stomping. Their mouths screaming obscenities. Their faces red with rage, but chancers, nonetheless. Carefully positioned just out of arm's reach. So many chancers, charlatans and cowards in this world. All living off the stories of others. Huh, we know who you are. Just as you do. But not all of course. Because keeping an arm's length is not an option for truly violent men.

And they were there too, those violent men within *their* ranks. Those who know you can survive the beatings, the batterings, the bleeding and the bruising. And they watched, and they knew to wait, for this was not the time. But the chancers amongst them, they sang:

'WHO ARE YA? ... WHO ARE YA? ...'

Though they knew who we were. And what we would have done, if only our arms could have stretched that far. Now you may well be thinking, is that any way to spend a Saturday afternoon? Admittedly, it's not for everyone. But to be fair, I wasn't the only one present now was I? I wasn't the only one that felt as I felt. So don't make the mistake of thinking that I am alone! We are many. It is not myself who is lost.

But it is just there, on a Saturday, a Tuesday, or maybe even a Wednesday. Or Thursday these days, come to think of it. But it is there and then, surrounded by like-minded individuals, that I like to indulge myself. Actually that's not one hundred percent true, if I'm honest. But you know what I mean. Obviously, you've got to be able to justify the reason for such outrageous behaviour, for such shenanigans. But when there is good reason, like, I don't know, say that *pikey* fella I mentioned earlier, remember? That one in the toilet. That fella with his cock in his hand. That one of three, with *not a pint of Guinness between them!* Because come on, if you didn't get it earlier, you surely must by now? Even *you* have to admit, he deserved that? I mean, what a filthy, nasty, cunt of a man. Nailing some poor fella's innocent little dog to a door for fuck's sake! What kind of sick bastard does something like that, eh? And when I say *pikey*, I do mean pikey. And I make no excuse for such a word. For he was not a *traveller,* as some daft cunts prefer we call them these days. He was a *pikey!* The type that only travel when the filth are on their case.

And so no, most definitely not a *traveller*. For travellers are fine. As are gypsies. True gypsies I might add. But no, I'm talking about the type of cock wipe that knocks on some grandad's door and offers to do his driveway for three grand and then demands five. Scaring the living shit out of the poor old bastard, leaving him shaking in his own home. Fearful of the next knock, knock, knock on the door. Or a car engine pulling up outside at two in the morning. The kind who'll threaten to put an old man's windows through if he doesn't pay up. Who'll mouth off at some poor old dear. Or torch their motor. Or, nail, a fucking dog, to a door! Those cunts! As I said, the type of arseholes daft white middle-class pricks, who've probably never suffered at their hands insist we now call *travellers* for fear of offence! *OFFENCE?* ... For fuck's sake!

No. I know exactly what I meant. He, that fella with his dick in his hand. The one staring straight ahead, as, men, do. He was scum. Just a cunt that needed his cock slicing so that he couldn't breed, and groom, and destroy an innocent child into thinking, and living the same way that he had chosen to live. That is of course, if he had a choice? Because you never know, he too might have suffered before I got to him. But still, I did us all a favour. You, me and the child he'll now never have. But as I say, it's mostly there, on a Saturday, a Tuesday, Wednesday, or even a Thursday these days, that I truly get to live.

But why? Why this desire to kick, to punch, to rage and destroy, not only others but myself?

Because it's fun, that's why. Pure and simple. Fun, fun, fucking fun. Something so dangerous. So unpredictable. Never knowing if I will win or lose. It sets you free. And deep down you, like me, must surely wish to be free. Free from the shitty drip, drip, drip of it all. And though I am sure you would find a different way, a much more wholesome way, to have such a feeling flooding through your veins, well, be honest, it must make you wonder?

19

Eventually, the police moved us on and into the stadium, where the sweet odour of over-priced shitty food and beer farts filled my senses. Football! This love. This way of life. This religion for which we live. She has such a hold on us. Through my time many loves will come and go, but not this one. From this one there is no retreat. More than any other she will bring me to my knees. She will tear my heart in two and have me cursing a million curses. But if ever I find myself to be judged, hers is the faith on which you should place my hand. And yet I am forced to share her. And in truth I love those I am forced to share her with, this love from which there is no turning. And as one we gather and we stand at her feet. Us worshippers, all equal, whether paupers or kings, three lads on a train. This glorious love. And yet there are those that believe they can own her. Those fools in dark suits with their money and egos. They despise the likes of me, of us. And rightly so of course! They despise us because they know the danger we pose. For we are watching them. And we judge them, just as they judge us.

Who are these clowns? Why are they even here, trying to win the affection of people they know nothing about? People they have nothing in common with, and never will? The arrogance they display in thinking our love, our support, our devotion is for sale. How dare they put a price on such loyalty, such love? These things, they are born to you. It is in your blood. If you want to know us, if you truly want to understand us, then come stand at our side. Come sing as we sing. Come give yourself, as we give ourselves. But no, they sit there, in their high places, looking down upon the likes of us. But their money buys them nothing but mistrust. How can they not see that? They know nothing of these streets, or of the communities and people this love of ours represents. How dare they think their money can take that from us.

To them such things are toys. A plaything to parade in front of their friends. A cock extension to wank off in the faces of rivals and enemies. Their egos driven by television deals and the adulation of invisible faces in bars from Boston to Beijing. Those fans that come but once a year for *the matchday experience*. The trippers who'll buy the shirt, the shorts, the socks, scarf, gloves, t-shirts, pants, dressing gowns etc, et-fucking-cetera. Anything that can be dreamed up to squeeze as much out of them as is humanly possible. Those pricks who come and film the match on their phones to prove to their friends that they were there, rather than actually *being* there. That's what they want. Not us. Not those that can see the whites of their eyes, week in week out. But still we come, rain or shine. We are the ones that will always keep her heart beating no matter how far she falls. And we will be there long after these thieves have gone.

And they bleed us dry. And they feast off our devotion. This loyalty, a love they will never come to feel or begin to understand. And they take, and they take. But we are watching them. And we are waiting. And so fear us they should. And we sang:

'WHO THE FUCKING HELL ARE YOU? ... WHO THE FUCKING HELL ARE YOU? ...'

Floodlights masked the darkening sky. And the clock ticked down. And then with the ninety minutes almost done, a long ball wide and over the top, and we were away. And my heart, it pounded. Defenders pulled, and they pushed, and they jostled for position, just as we did. A stepover, once, twice. A dip of the shoulder. A few precious inches gained, and that ball, it was sent curling into the box. A flash of bright white caught against the yellowy glow of those lights. Their keeper came and then stopped. And my heart held its breath. That flash of white. The header. A bullet onto the underside of the bar that shot down and then up, up into the roof of that net. And the keeper, he hit the ground, beaten. And in that moment, that brief moment of my time on this earth, she drowned us all in her glory.

Ohhhhh you beauty! That rush, that elation. When the love we so gratefully give is so beautifully rewarded. This is why as one we follow her. This is why we devote our lives to her, us paupers and kings. Oh, and the pain it caused them! A lucky few made the lush green turf in celebration. Police scurried to help the yellow-bibbed stewards as they struggled to keep control. And the coins they rained down upon us. I watched as one of theirs jumped the barrier, incensed by those who had dared set foot upon their hallowed turf, his mouth spitting rage, his face tormented and torn. Stewards grabbed and pulled. Police dragged him to the floor. They pinned, and they cuffed him. And as they took him away, we sang:

'WANKER ... WANKER ... WANKER ...'

Oh to be consumed with such anger, such hatred. Have you ever cared that much about anything? Cared as much as that lad did at that moment? I love and understand him more than I ever will those who live their lives on their phones. Their existence blurred by social media. Craving *likes* from strangers with fake tans and false tits. Brainwashed by the mind-numbing drip, drip, drip feeding of what they should look like, should feel like, and aspire to be, without ever reaching inside themselves to find out who they *truly* are. That lad, his mouth spitting. His arms struggling to free himself from the clutches of those that have chosen to control him. Him, I understand. Him, I know as well as I know myself. And what I would have given just for the chance to go toe to toe with him, to feel his pain. And we sang:

'ONE-NIL ... ONE-NIL ... ONE-NIL ... ONE-NIL ...'

Oh for such days, for they are few and far between. And as the clock ticked and it tocked, and we celebrated our win, they gave it one last punt. And for some reason our defence, they stood still. And their number ten, he was left alone. He raced in on our goal. Our keeper came to meet him. And the stadium drew its breath. It fell silent - As it does at such moments. And that ten of theirs, he opened his chest. And he curled that ball around an outstretched leg. And then it came to rest, in the back of that net. And the locals, they went mental - As of course you would at such a sight. And all I could do was stand. And watch. And take it. Oh, and they gave it. They properly gave it some. And my eyes, they narrowed. And I watched those dirty, northern, paupers and kings dance their dance.

How many times? How many more, fucking times,

eh? It was less than a minute, not even one, fucking, minute! I fucking hate football! And I stood, and I watched. And then she lifted my head once more. And in some perverse way I began to enjoy their dance. For she had reminded me ... They will never be us.

20

I've always considered myself a lucky man. Lucky in life. The people I've met, the girlfriends I've had, well mostly. Sure, there have been a few that, looking back on it, I'd have probably given a swerve, had I known. And I've no doubt there'll be a few thinking the very same about yours truly. But in general, I've been very lucky. I've seen things others will never see. Sought out adventure and escaped scrapes that would have dragged many other men down. I've felt alive, that I've lived. And I know I've lived, because I see so many dead people walking. Their clocks ticking as they go about their pointless existence. Slowly plodding until their legs fail them, and their walk is over. Don't get me wrong, I've met my fair share of pricks; the liars, crooks, and thieves. Some by chance, others much closer to home. You can forgive people once, maybe even twice, but three times? ... No.

And I know I've fucked up many, many times myself and thankfully been forgiven. But there comes a time when you have to say enough is enough, accept it and release yourself from those that feed off you. And when you do that, when you let go, all you are left with are those you can truly trust. Belonging is a strange thing. That sense that you really belong to someone, something, to this world! Like I said, I am lucky. I have never felt alone. Even at the beginning. Our mothers, fathers, sisters, and brothers, all loved - well mostly. Their blood in ours.

But they are just people. Important people no doubt. The ones that shape you more than any other, but still, just people. Some friends, great friends even, Others most certainly not. Each with their own lives. Their own thoughts. Their own desires. Their gifts and their failings, just as I have mine. They say blood is thicker than water, but I've seen plenty of blood, and the blood I've seen belongs to people I've met along the way. People I know I can trust. And though few in number, they are the most loyal. I was not born to them, but I am certain I was born one of them. There are no excuses for me. It's too easy to blame this, or to point a finger at that. But for me there really are none.

Not for the way I am and the path I walk. Some of us are just as we were born. As we were set down here to be. And along the way, if we are lucky, we find others like us.

And like I say, I consider myself, a very lucky man.

21

The police marched us back to the station. And as we made our way, those northern lads, they came to give us their send-off. And what a send-off it was. Good lads one and all. Lads to whom I would lift my hat, if it was not there to hide my face. And as the bottles spun past my head. And with glass shattering at my feet. And with the clip-clopping of horses in my ears, the snapping and snarling of dogs at my ankles, and the whirling of sirens buzzing around my head, I, I my friend am more alive than you could ever possibly imagine. For at such moments, I find myself to be the man I truly know myself to be. The man I was set down here to be. A proper little cunt! Surrounded by like-minded little cunts!

And so, while others wander around furniture

stores picking out pictures of stones. Or buying packets of candles to enhance that treasured wank in the bath. Or worse still sit at home on their fat arses watching has-beens and wannabes eating kangaroo cocks! Or voting for karaoke singers with stories of dead dads and lost friends, I, I have the smell of blood in my nostrils. I have its taste on my tongue and its dampness on my knuckles. Oh, the beauty of violence, and the freedom it brings. For at such moments nothing else matters! Nothing else exists! Imagine that. The weight of it all, lifted from your shoulders for a few, short, minutes? Surely you can see, that *has* to be worth the odd kick in the bollocks?

It all got a bit out of hand, if truth be told. It usually does when we come to town. A copper was pulled from his horse. And as he fell backwards the horse bolted, and that copper's leg got caught in the stirrups. And he was dragged along, his head bouncing off the tarmac. Nasty that, proper nasty.

22

Sometimes, when I'm feeling lost. Lost, or empty. Empty's a good word. Yeah empty, when my head is, empty, I'll go and sit on the hill overlooking the park and just stare back across the valley at the flats opposite. And for a few hours I'll sit, and I'll wonder to myself just what must be going on within the eighteen floors of each of those three horrendous concrete monstrosities. Nighttime is best, when the lights are on. No-one knows what goes on behind closed doors and pulled curtains - The lives and the lies that people front, their secrets. Huh, everyone wants to know a secret eh. And I'll sit, and I can't help but imagine that behind those curtains there'll be lovers. Some for the first time, some for the hundredth, but still lovers nonetheless.

There'll be happy families curled up on sofas

watching television, or sharing the joy and laughter of their day. Children will be tucked-in tight, being read stories by those that would happily lay down their lives for them. I've no doubt both the young and old would be sleeping, some lost in the beauty of their dreams. Maybe travelling to faraway places. Or better still, once more walking hand in hand with those they've loved and since lost. The beauty and the wonder of what we lies deep inside. Deep, deep down in those places of which we ourselves are unaware. Of our imagination, our, soul.

But nearby will lie the dregs. The pimps, the pushers and the pervs. Those that prey on the addicted and the vulnerable. There'll be the bullies and the abusers. The abused and the defeated. The world in all its beautiful and ugly glory. All encased in concrete. The good, the bad and the unsightly. The hopeful and the diseased. All living above, beneath and alongside one another, blissfully unaware of what breathes just feet away. It's funny when you think about it. Well it would be, if it wasn't true! And it'll be happening tonight and every night, in those flats. As it will be in such buildings here, there and every fucking where!

Still, at least there will be the lovers, eh! Well, you'd hope so! Because if not, why are we even here?

23

On the journey south we kept our heads down and sat well away from the pack. A wise move as the Old Bill boarded at various stations in the hope of picking out faces filmed and photographed from earlier. Once back in London we distanced ourselves further still by bowling our way over from Euston to Warren Street Underground. And my mind, it spun from here to there, from this to that. A heady mix of powder, pills, and alcohol, both paid for and stolen from the train's buffet car. And what a feeling, what a feeling I had about me as I made my way down the escalator to the Northern Lines southbound platform.

London! London on a Saturday night. All those faces. All those nationalities. Each and every one of them, loved by one, despised by at least one other.

We're a strange breed us humans. Who knows what draws or repels us from one another? All I know is that I could live down there, in the underground. With my head spinning. Just watching mind. Just watching. Deep in the belly of that city.

You've got to love London. So many people. All shapes, sizes, shades and persuasions. And yet the trippers, they say Londoners are cold. Not that they've ever tried to meet one of course. And I mean a proper Londoner, be they white, black, yellow or brown; if indeed I can say such a thing? Because they all head there, to that *unfriendly* place. From all four corners of this earth, they head. And they settle in that city so many believe to be so unwelcoming. And they put down their roots. And they have their families, all now Londoners as much as any. There, in that place, so many dismiss.

Those outsiders who visit. The day-outs and weekenders. Who see London as no more than the cut-down tube map, Where the Victoria Line ends at Finsbury Park, and the Central ends at Ealing. The map on which Wimbledon, Barnet and Mile End cease to exist. And yet still they come. And they think they know London and its people. And they brush shoulders with the other visitors. And they see what they came to see. And they go back home and say Londoners are u*nfriendly*, even though they never really took the time to talk, to ask, to find out. Because when they come they keep themselves to themselves. And they chat with their pals. And they dine with their partners, in that most *unfriendly* of places.

But if you could have stopped that tube, as it snaked its path in the very pit of that city. Frozen it, and removed all of those that were not born, that do not live, work or indeed had now settled in that, that most *unfriendly* of places, then, well, we'd still not have got a seat, eh! Not with all the trippers: - *'Not that I wanted one. A seat that is!'* - Not with all that gear flowing through my veins: - *'The last thing I needed was a seat. I could have done with a shit!'* - My head from here to there. I'm just saying. Londoners! When did any of them last even try? Before heading back home, and telling of just how *unfriendly* London is ... But still they come. And it is they, as much as any, that make it the place they so eagerly believe it to be.

That said, I wouldn't blame anyone for not wanting to go to Tottenham Hale. Now there's a proper shit hole if ever there were!

24

The sliding doors of the tube train closed us in. And as we headed off, the rat-a-tat-tat of that train on the tracks mixed with the dirty warm air that blew in through the carriage's adjoining window. And my mind, it raced from here to there, to this to that, and I thought of a million other things besides. And just as darkness had encased us, light began to seep in, signalling our arrival into the next station. As we entered, shapes on the platform turned to faces. Groups of men and women on a night out. Couples, and the lonely. The brakes hit for the first time, forcing an old man back down into his seat. He apologised to those he thought bothered enough to care, but this was London, the visitors and trippers London on a Saturday night, and so no-one did. And as we slowed, a group of men were passed, their eyes caught, a sudden sight of movement:

''Ere, did you see those fellas on the platform back there?' asked Ryan.

I think it was Ryan.

And as we slowed, and we slowed, a lad suddenly appeared running alongside the carriage. A lad desperate to catch up. A lad with a pointy face. A bony, ratty-looking face. A face etched with madness. A face I'll never forget. A face I shall undoubtedly now take to my grave. And as he came bouncing alongside, that ratty-looking fella announced his arrival by smacking *HARD* on the window. Passengers jolted. Heads turned:

''Ere, check this cunt out!' said Darren.

I'm pretty sure it was Darren who said that! And as we came to a stop, more appeared at Ratty's side ... five ... ten ... fifteen:

'Fucking hell lads, looks like we're on here!' said Philbs.

I am one hundred percent certain it was Philbs who said that! ... And the driver of that train announced:

'GOODGE STREET STATION ... THE NEXT STATION STOP IS GOODGE STREET STATION.'

Funny how it can all just turn. If only we'd not walked from Euston. Or we'd caught an earlier tube! Or the one behind even! But if you play the game, well

I suppose these things are bound to catch up with you from time to time.

The sliding doors of the carriage opened, unleashing a barrage of violent abuse that sent us back. Passengers dashed for cover. And the screams of the girls and the boys on a night out clashed with the violent bile directed our way:

'COME ON THEN YOU COCKNEY BASTARDS … LET'S FUCKING HAVE IT … COME ON YA FUCKERS.'

And it was at that point I realised that those standing before me, those men so intent on having their way, that they were: - *'Brummies!'* - Which took me back, if I'm honest. I don't know why, but it just wasn't what I was expecting! Though what I was, expecting I mean, I don't know. My head all over the shop. But not Brummies: – *'That's weird!'* - I thought. For: - *'It is a funny accent that, even at the best of times eh! Which this most certainly wasn't.'* - I thought: - *'One that's hard to take seriously, especially when being so, aggressive.'* - But those lads with violence on their minds, Brummies they most certainly were. And they clearly thought they recognised us from somewhere. From some tear-up or another. Well they must have done, because we hadn't said a word up until that point.

And as they came at us, space opened up. Outnumbered, we sought the safety of the carriage. While they, those Brummie lads, so intent on having their way darted backwards and forward. And they bounced from toe to toe:

'COME ON YOU COCKNEY BASTARDS ... FIGHT ... FUCKING FIGHT.'

And I kept thinking: - *'But we're not Cockneys! What's with all this Cockney bollocks?'* - And for the life of me I just could not place where it was that we must have met! Though clearly they thought we had. At some match or another. And then there it was, that sudden glint of steel:

'D'YOU WANT A PIECE OF THIS, EH? ... COME ON YA COCKNEY BASTARD.'

'But we're not Cockneys!' - I wanted to tell him: - *'Are you sure you've not made a mistake?'* - I wanted to ask. My head, it really was all over the shop. And that glint of steel it flashed past Keith, sending him scuttling backwards. It opened even more space between us, a no man's land into which Ratty stepped. And he jabbed and he sliced at thin air. Others followed, their arms swinging and their boots kicking: - *'And there was me looking forward to a nice night out on the town with the boys.'* - If only he didn't have that blade! But have that blade he did. And he jabbed and he sliced.

The cold nick of steel went almost unnoticed. The arm of Keith's shirt cut. For Ratty seemed to have a fix on Keith for some reason. Fuck knows why! Philbs landed a boot into Ratty's thigh, sending him down to one knee. Another kick landed square in his back … And the driver announced:

'THIS TRAIN IS ABOUT TO DEPART … PLEASE STAND CLEAR OF THE CLOSING DOORS … THIS TRAIN IS ABOUT TO DEPART … THANK YOU.

And with those doors closing, Ratty's friends pulled him back out onto the platform. Shame really. If only we could have kept him there, inside with us. What a whole lot of grief that would have saved. Not for him of course! Well maybe, looking back on it.

Blood stained Keith's shirt. It seeped through the cloth and dripped to the floor of that carriage, though Keith didn't notice. And those doors, for some reason, they reopened … And the driver announced:

'LADIES AND GENTLEMEN, CAN YOU PLEASE STAND CLEAR OF THE CLOSING DOORS … THIS TRAIN IS READY TO DEPART … PLEASE STAND CLEAR OF THE DOORS.

It must have been someone further up the train. Some prick with a foot in the door. Some voyeur keen to see what was happening. Captivated by the violence. A nobody. Another one of those fucking chancers, filming it all on his or her phone. Desperate to share on Facebook. Or to sell to some tabloid for fifty poxy quid and that all important name check. You never know, they might even get their face on Sky shitty News with this one! Three or four of their fifteen so-called minutes of fame. If only they knew the grief they would cause! If only they'd have let those doors close shut, so that we could have all been on our merry way. But those doors, they did indeed open ... And the driver announced:

'FOLKS, CAN YOU PLEASE KEEP AWAY FROM THE DOORS ... WE CAN'T MOVE OFF UNTIL THE DOORS ARE CLOSED ... PLEASE STAND CLEAR OF THE DOORS.'

Two lads darted forward. They pulled and tugged at Keith, desperate to get him out onto the platform. Keith being Keith fought back, but pull and tug they did, and out onto the platform Keith went. And those doors, they slammed shut. And all we could do was watch. As up popped that ratty-faced looking fella ... And slice ... Keith's face tore open. A freshly-cut void of flesh ... And slice: – *'Poor Keith. Poor Julie! Keith's Julie that is. I mean, he was never the best-looking fella in the world, but fuck me, she was not going to be happy once she saw that!'* - ... And slice ... Like a freshly cut ribbon of raw red cabbage, it was ... And slice ... Blood splattered the windows. Screams fill the carriage ... And slice ... Like ribbon, after ribbon of freshly cut red raw cabbage ... And that driver announced:

'LADIES AND GENTLEMEN, PLEASE STAND CLEAR OF THE DOORS ... WE'VE ALL GOT PLACES AND HOMES TO GO TO, BUT WE CAN'T BE ON OUR WAY UNTIL THE DOORS ARE CLOSED.'

And once again those doors, those beautiful doors, they opened, and so out we went. Faces appeared from further up and down the train, faces known, but names not. And as the violence erupted around me well, that ratty faced little fucker, in a world of his own he was! I planted a right hander square into the side of Ratty's head, and down he went: – *'One punch! Again, one punch was all it took to end it! Poor Keith and limp lettuce.'* - The blade spun from Ratty's hand. It slid along the platform and down onto the tracks. And as Ratty tried to lift himself and make for the exit, I decided to help him on his way with a size eight up the arse. And as the boots and the fists flew, I followed Ratty. And just as he got to that exit, I grabbed the hair on that bony, ratty head of his, and I RAMMED it into that wall ... FUCK ME! ... The beautiful sensation that only violent revenge can bring. That joyful pleasure, his bones cracking shuddering up my arm ... as OVER, AND OVER, AND OVER ... And the train that had brought us there, it was gone, oblivious. And as I turned Ratty's face a yellowy red mush, his blood staining my skin that glorious shade of claret, I suddenly picked up on the rumbly rumble of the next train as it snaked its way down the tracks from High Barnet to Morden: – *'Well I say Morden, it could have been terminating at Kennington for all I knew.'* - From here to there. From this to that: - *'I mean the fucking nerve of that fella cutting poor Keith like that!*

And as I looked up to see the light of that train illuminating the tunnel, for there was no turning back. I decided to drag that blob at my feet out onto that platform. And a right old mess it left: - *'A proper ruby red path for some poor cog on minimum wage to clean up.'* – I thought: - *'A good couple of hours that'll take.'* - My head all over the shop, it was. And as I dragged him to where so many innocents had stood, just waiting, and waiting, and waiting. I looked up to see horror etched on to that driver's face. That poor driver who was about to be forever scarred by what she saw before her.

And I know I shouldn't have thought it, but I thought it nonetheless, that it was indeed a woman driving that train!: – *'Well who'd have fucking thought it!'* - I thought, amongst all that: – *'A woman driving a tube train!'* - And then just as quickly: – *'Well why wouldn't it be? Why shouldn't it be? A woman? Just another one of us cogs. Who, like we all do, day in and out, probably headed off to work that morning, just wanting the minutes to pass. So that she could return home to her family ... If indeed she had one.'* – I thought: - *'Or just a husband. Or boyfriend. Or girlfriend even!'* - Funny eh, nurse! I said Ron, he's funny aint he?

And as she drew closer, Wrong place wrong time: – *'Who might have kids, or might not?'* – Mind all over the shop. Closer, and closer. That poor, poor woman. Just another one of those beautiful, loving, kind, giving creatures us filthy, rotten, twisted, perverted fucking men take for granted. Our mothers, our sisters. Our wives, our daughters. The whores and the tarts we meet in bars. As they meet us, let's not forget! Some of whom tell such vile lies. And I do say *some*. Many of whom play the game, just as men do. And yes, I do say, and mean many! But not that one. Not that poor woman who was about to be forever scarred. And as she drew closer: – *'Poor Keith and dead cats, and blood spilt over Kebabs.'* - And with that mess at my feet, on that platform edge: – *'Three lads on a train. Red cabbage and squashed chips. And Keith's bloodied face.'* - And the rumble and screeeeech: – *'And ribbon, after ribbon, after ribbon of freshly cut red raw cabbage.'* - I yanked hard. And I spun that fucker around. And BOSH. It was done. Just, like, that ... Ducks and air pistols.

25

Something must have woke me. A slight movement? Something accidently knocked. Or instinct, maybe. I'm a light sleeper at the best of times, but I must have heard something. She was out cold. Always was. She slept heavy. A dead weight for such a slight, beautiful, delicate thing. I could feel her there though. I loved that. I needed the contact. Just the slightest of touch. A finger laid on her skin. Or my foot lightly resting against hers. Something, just so I knew she was there. That I wasn't, alone.

Then BANG, BANG, BANG. The front door came crashing in. My first reaction was: - *'Fuck me, the post-man's keen!'* - She screamed. Well you would, wouldn't you? Though that said, I didn't. To be fair, I suppose deep down I was expecting them. Come to think of it, I'm surprised it took them so long! Then:

'POLICE … POLICE … BLAH, BLAH, BLAH …'

And all the other bollocks they spout at such moments. Obviously I'm out of bed like a fucking rocket. Standing there, stark bollock naked. I can't wear anything in bed you see, not even pants. Haven't done since I was about, I don't know, ten maybe. Well there's no need is there. Not if you've got a decent duvet. A fifteen or twenty tog, depending on the time of year. I've never liked Jimmy Jams. Waste of money in my opinion. If I'm staying round someone's house, or sharing a room on a jolly with the lads, I'll keep my undies on out of respect and that. Especially if Iffy's about! But in my own place? No, no jammies. No, nothing.

She had hers on, obviously! I don't know how she did it. Every night wrapped up like a fucking eskimo. And thank fuck she did, have them on, I mean, considering! Because by then she was out of bed too. In the corner, standing there, holding the duvet over herself. Poor thing. Shitting a brick she was. Eyes bulging, shouting something. Fuck knows what! Shaking and screaming. Bouncing up and down like a fucking yoyo. Not knowing whether to stand or sit. In sheer panic, she was. It wasn't right, not really, she didn't deserve that. And from the other side of the door I'm hearing:

'POLICE … GET DOWN ON THE FLOOR … WE'RE COMING IN.'

And I'm standing there thinking: - *'Well come in then! I've half been expecting ya!'* - And so I shout:

'COME IN THEN, NO ONE'S STOPPING YA!'

And suddenly the door comes crashing in off its hinges. And I couldn't help think: - *'Well there was no need for that now was there? I said 'come in' didn't I?' And now I'm going to have to fix that. And that'll cost a good few quid that will, fixing that!'* - I thought: – *'A fair few bob that'll be!'* - And in they piled, one after another. No 'hello', 'good morning sir, how's it going?', no nothing. They just piled in. And I mean, it really was a good job she had her Jimmy Jams on, eh!

Because for all they knew we could have been at it. Clattering into each other like a couple of dirty dogs. Or slowly, gently, making love. Holding onto each other. Hands searching. Lips placing gentle kisses. No words. Just the sound of the pleasure we both lovingly gave and received. Although to be fair, we wouldn't have been, at it, I mean. Not since the weekend any way. Because I'd had quite a lot on my mind, to be honest. What with everything.

And they bundled me to the floor. Again, no need for it really, because, as I said, I'd invited them in: *'Come in then',* I'd said - well shouted actually. And one of them has a knee in my back. And others have theirs pushing hard into my legs and thighs. And someone, one of the bastards was ramming my face into the floor as hard as he, or she, could. Well you never know these days do ya? It could just as easily have been a *she*, doing the ramming: - *'For we all like a bit of the old in and out.'* – I thought. And once down there I couldn't help but think: - *'Fuck me, this carpet needs a clean!'* - Which were strange, because I'd only done it a few days before. Christ only knows how it gets so dirty. I don't mind hoovering, hoovering and washing up. It relaxes me. Used to do it with my mum: - *'Dear old mum. Her back to me, standing at the sink.'*

And then the old handcuffs went on. But the knees they kept pressing. Those nasty little piggies, inflicting so much pain. Pain that'll leave no mark, apart from the odd bruise or two maybe. Because that's what they do. For we all play the game. And then I'm lifted up and sat on the bed, knackers swinging. And I saw that it wasn't a *she* after all, ramming my face into that dirty carpet. Which was a good job really, as I wasn't looking my best down there, what with the sudden visit we'd just received; my poor, beautiful, delicate girl and I. And then they led her away, out into another room, and I shouted to her:

'It's okay love, don't worry.'

And she's was shouting fuck knows what back. I couldn't really focus, what with my tackle hanging out. And then in walks the top copper and, wallop, I'm given the nod as to what it was all about. Like I didn't kind of know already. And then boom:

'You're nicked my son.'

But before they took me away, I asked to have some pants put on me. In order to hide my modesty and all that. And as that copper eased them on, because they refused to take the cuffs off, for some reason! As he eased those blue boxers over my big fat white arse, I leaned in, and I blew hard in his earhole. He jolted. And the others, those other piggies, they clearly thought I'd bit him. That I'd had a cheeky little nibble on his lughole, and so they began to beat the fuck out of me. And I could hear her screaming. Because all she could hear was them going to town on her poor defenceless boy. Which was really kind of her considering! Kind that she still cared. That she could even entertain the thought of giving a flying fuck about me, after what I'd just put her through.

But I did not bite, I just blew, blew in that ear of his. I made sure I didn't leave a mark. Though at that moment they most certainly left theirs. Oh, they left plenty, both black and blue. And you know what? I didn't really mind. Always thinking me. Always thinking.

26

'Food's ready to go. ... JOE ... I SAID, FOOD'S REA...'

'ALRIGHT, I'M COMING! Fucking hell!'

It's funny how things turn out, eh? All that must be what, eighteen months, two years ago maybe. I lose track, if truth be told. But then again, when did truth ever come into it? Now there's a lie if ever there were, *The Truth*!

You see, they spend a lifetime moulding and manipulating you into being part of their game, and so surely, should the need arise, you'd be a fool not to play. Oh, and I played. We all did. My lawyer, she played a blinder - Yeah, I know. Us boys and girls. Us liars and cheats.

Obviously, we didn't tell them about the football. Well, they didn't need to hear all that now did they? -

Mums being mums and everything! The story went, well … We'd just been up north, to Blackpool, Your Honour. Stag do. Celebrating the coming marriage of my best mate Keith to his beloved Julie - Not that Keith and Julie were getting married, of course. But you find out who your friends are at times such as that. Good old Julie.

I was down to be Keith's best man, what with him being my oldest mate and all that! I mean, I've known Keith since I was a dot. Virtually spent all my youth around his house, especially the summer holidays, what with my own home life being so rough. Mum and dad constantly beating me as they did - *Oh to abuse a child and the scars that leaves!* Broke their hearts hearing that. But again, needs must, eh!

And it would appear that our drinks may well have been spiked on that train journey back. Probably Iffy, what with him having previous and that. And let's face it, enough gear turned up in Keith's blood. What was left of it! And I really do recall not quite feeling myself on that train journey home, my head from here to there, to this to that. I can only assume it must have been the drugs. And what with me never having taken any before! As I testified on that good book of yours - What with me being a believer and everything! 'Your Honour,' I said, to that most honourable of gents, sat there looking down upon me. With the power to judge, to believe, and to be deceived.

And I held my hands up, for admittedly I may well have got a little carried away, that I agreed. But seeing your best mate getting sliced up like that! And what with the drink and the drugs, well, that's enough to send anyone over the edge, I'd say! Wouldn't you, Your Honour?

And let's not forget that ratty-faced fella, well he came at us remember? Slicing and cutting. Cutting and slicing. In truth I was just defending myself. And everyone else in that carriage, to be fair. As that good woman got up to testify on my behalf. I mean, according to her I deserved a medal! But who am I to judge? - My judge.

And that man sat there looked down upon me. Just another one of those so-called great and good. Many of whom are just as twisted and perverted as any they pass judgement upon. Who lie, and who cheat, and cover each other's backs just as we do! Who let guilty friends walk free. Who undervalue those we value most. Desert our old and dismiss the vulnerable. Nearly all of whom happily send our young men and women to wars based on lies, to keep their fingers buried in such lucrative pies. And so I question: - *'Which will it be, my most Dishonourable Gent?'* - Hook line and sinker: - *'Do you believe my lies as much as we have to endure yours?'*

And when they can't quite make up their minds, they stick you in front of some other fool. Some egotistical prick, who's read a few books, and collected a few letters after his or her name. Just one more pathetic soul, who no doubt at times is just as fearful and scarred as any they sit opposite. And that person sat there, they will question and probe, and they'll search for an excuse. And that person sat there they'll prod, and they'll tug, trying to dig out some secret - *Everyone wants to know a secret eh!* - Just as you have done from the moment I mentioned it: *'If I told you a secret, would you use it against me?'* Or indeed I against you?

And so, with the game in full flow, and when the timing is just right, that person sat opposite, you throw them a bone. And you sit and you watch as that ego kicks in. And when the timing's just right, you then throw them another. And when the timing's just right, you throw them one more. Until after just a few short hours, that person sat opposite thinks they know all about you. And you watch as they sit back, basking in the glory of themselves, and prepare to pass their verdict. Just as you will do. A verdict inevitably influenced by their own hopes and desires. Their triumphs and failures. Their fears and misgivings, quirks and perversions. On whether or not they tasted the sweet sticky juice of a woman on their tongue last night. Or felt cock in hand, in mouth or inside last week, last month, or last year. Because it's funny what a bit of the old in-and-out can do for one's mood, eh! - If indeed you're lucky enough to be getting any that is! And then that person sat opposite, they'll take out their pen, they'll write you a label, and then they hide you away.

But what if there are no secrets? Sometimes there simply are no excuses. Surely by now you must see that some of us are just how we were set down here to be? Us boys and girls. So many liars and cheats - Thc lies and lives that people front. Paths so easily laid and yet so egotistically followed - *Ducks and air pistols?* ... For fuck sake!

Make no mistake, a violent man will always find a fight. A nutter will always find someone to nut. It's either in you or it isn't. This world! So many charlatans. So many fools, so easily fooled!

If you give the likes of me a way out, do you honestly think I'm too stupid not to take it? - Fourteen years there, or four or five here? Always thinking me, eh! And so, those precious letters after those names of yours, you keep them. Keep them for someone who truly needs them. For with me, and so many like me, it really is quite simple. Sometimes, and I do say *some*, I'm a bit of a cunt:

'Are you okay Joe?'

'Oh, you made me proper jump there sister. Yes, I'm fine thank you. I just got a little lost in my thoughts for a bit. And you?

'I'm good thank you. And thanks for asking.'

'Sister, I hope you don't mind me saying, but having the news on the television all day long, all the bad stuff it beams in. All that, unhappiness. It can't be helping any of the people in here?'

'That's a good point Joe. I'll get one of the porters to turn it over.'

And with that she turns and she leaves. I stand and I watch her go. And then me, being, me, well:

'And sister.'

'Yes Joe?'

'I hope you don't mind me saying, but I really like what you've done with your hair.'

I see a smile cross her lips. A slight redness brighten in her cheeks. And with no words needed, she turns once more and heads away. Where would we be without such, love?

Well, I suppose I should get the rest of these meals out, eh:

'So, what do you want, the soup, or the fish?'

ABOUT THE AUTHOR

Eddy Brimson is an award-winning comedian, bestselling author, actor, and documentary maker.

Eddy became a professional comedian in 2000, quickly establishing himself as one of the most sought-after headline acts on both the UK and International stand-up circuits. His career has taken him from Yeovil to Yangon, Scunthorpe to Shanghai. He is also a regular on the world festival circuit, having performed solo shows in New Zealand, Australia, The Alps, and of course the greatest festival of all, Edinburgh.

Previously Eddy had penned six bestselling sports books based around football fan culture: four co-written, alongside two solo titles. He has also previously written one novel: the critically acclaimed *Hooligan.*

His books have been translated into both Russian and Italian, with worldwide sales to date exceeding 700,000.

As an actor Eddy has numerous TV and film credits to his name. However, *Naughty Boy* the play, is his first solo project.

Eddy has also written produced and presented two

documentaries following The England National Football Team: Teargas and Tantrums in 1998. And: Some People Don't Get Football, I Don't Get Those People in 2012.

Born in Hemel Hempstead in 1964, Eddy is the youngest of six children. Football mad from the moment he could kick a ball he follows Watford FC. His hometown club, Hemel Hempstead Town FC. And of course, England. However, due to his life on the road as a comedian, he can usually be found on a Saturday visiting various non-league grounds.

Eddy is a keen animal lover and played a lead part in the National Anti-Hunting campaign, for whom he held the joint position of press officer for a brief spell. This led to him being under surveillance by Mi5 and his subsequent arrest at gunpoint on suspicion of terrorism. All charges were dropped.

Eddy can be contacted via his website:

www.eddybrimson.com

For clips of his work visit:

YouTube: Eddy Brimson

ALSO BY EDDY BRIMSON

Fiction:

Hooligan

Factual:

Teargas & Ticket Touts

God Save The Team

Co-written:

Everywhere We Go

England My England

Derby Days

Capital Punishment

Documentary titles:

Teargas & Tantrums

Some People Don't Get Football, I Don't Get Those People.

Printed in Great Britain
by Amazon

58930491R00083